Books by Harvey Havel:

Noble McCloud (1999)
The Imam (2000)
Freedom of Association (2006)
From Poets to Protagonists (2009)
Harvey Havel's Blog, Essays (2011)
Stories from the Fall of the Empire (2011)
Two Tickets to Memphis (2012)
Mother, A Memoir (2013)
Charlie Zero's Last-Ditch Attempt (2014)
The Orphan of Mecca, Book One (2016)
The Orphan of Mecca, Book Two (2016)
The Orphan of Mecca, Book Three (2016)
The Thruway Killers (2017)
Mister Big (2018)
The Wild Gypsy of Arbor Hill (2019)
A Rumination on the Role of Love during A Condition of
Extreme Conservativism and Extreme Liberalism,
A Political Essay (2019)

ISBN: 978-0578-49673-3

The Wild Gypsy of Arbor Hill

A Novella

By

Harvey Havel

For Bianca

"My Mistress is Nothing like the Sun..."

Chapter One

A love for a woman can possess a man in a sharp minute and make him play the fool just out of his fierce desire for her. For me, though, it takes hold slowly, as I have learned to love over the years. When we become mature, we realize that love operates in different ways. And I don't mean to sound patronizing here, but it comes upon us slowly until it hits us full blast, that sharp minute where the world stops turning. Such a feeling can last for ages, through time, like an endless ocean that swells on its own.

I am one of those people who have learned to love. I grew to care about the woman I knew from long ago, as I remember our situation well. I'm older now, and just looking back upon the woman I learned to love so deeply, I had little choice but to set her free. It was never going to work anyway. Her name was Gypsy, and she was a working girl, a woman of the night, a sex worker, a serious crack addict - well known for her thievery and long criminal rap sheet.

I think people should know, however, that I am a man from good stock. My family is from New England - New Hampshire to be specific. We are Protestants and as white as they come. Nevertheless, I've relied on inherited wealth to get by. We don't need jobs and probably won't for the rest of our lives. Through my grandfather, though, I have learned that the criminally corrupted grandfather makes it. The father manages it. And the spoiled child spends it all away. While this short dictum doesn't apply to me right now, I remember when my father's time had neared, and several years after his death, I became the sole beneficiary of his will.

Yes, my father loved me that much. He saw that I was properly educated at Exeter, and straight after that, I moved on to Trinity College in Connecticut. They let me in for my test scores, as my grades at Exeter were abysmal. I never really studied what they wanted me to study there. Back when I went to Exeter, though, they had the most gorgeous women on and off that pristine campus. And then they had a similar bunch of women who went to Trinity. In fact, I think they measured the curves of their bodies before they accepted them.

For my first two years at college, I went without a girlfriend, but when I became a bit taller, less of nerd, and a participant in athletics, the women looked at me differently. They began talking to me every once in a while, at the library. Some of them would say hello to me right out of the blue. How they talked to me felt awkward. For two years straight I had been ignored, and then suddenly, after I hit my Junior year, they turned around and noticed me.

It was an odd feeling - to be rejected and then suddenly accepted by them. I went through my first few years of college believing they didn't like me. I questioned it, because I didn't know why they didn't, but my internal thoughts of their dislike of me seemed to color everything I did at my old college. It also colored everything I did before I arrived at the college in Connecticut.

I tried to find out why they disliked me. I wanted to know why I was so excluded from their parties, their cliques, their wealth. I usually kept to myself. Maybe they saw that I was smart, both with aptitude and intellect, especially when I first arrived at Trinity. Maybe I didn't know the protocol involved when trying to hit on the young women there.

Generally, though, I avoided all of these tricky social games and just went through college where I actually learned something and applied myself to study instead of wasting it all away on booze, young women, and the constant show of wealth. I even wore strange clothing. Most of the students wore chinos and collared polo shirts. I wore plaid a few times, and because I was never a sucker for fashion or showing off my wealth, I guess they continued to ignore me. I am still unclear why. It all changed, though, especially when I joined the ice hockey team.

I never expected to thrive in hockey, but once I started to improve, the coach gave me more time on the ice. Some of the sorority women would watch the games, and maybe they were impressed by me. And that night, after a victory over Amherst, I went to the usual fraternity party, and it was there that a young, hot woman with curves in all the right places, asked if she could get me a beer.

The bar was crowded that night, so to be more gentlemanly, I requested that I should get her the beer. This is why the women must have disliked me. I was much too much of a gentleman, and slowly I was taking on the role of the traditional Protestant housewife, which was to give comfort to their men in times of need. I saw it completely then. It should have been the woman's prerogative to get me that beer. Instead, I, more polite than the woman in this case, just had to one-up her and get her the beer myself, thereby negating her purpose.

A big crowd had formed around the rim of the bar, and while I was not a fraternity brother there, the heavyweight behind the bar still let me in first and poured me a beer, half of which was foam. I asked him to pour me another one, and he did so without complaint. I brought the beer back to the same spot, but she was gone. I saw her in the corner away from the bar flirting with another man.

The guy who talked to her was a ruffian of sorts. He was tall and wore a leather jacket. He was on the football team, and in most cases, the football and ice hockey teams remained cordial and friendly to one another. I didn't really care that she talked to him, but I knew right then and there that a lot of pretty women actually liked being treated like shit. From what I could overhear, the guy was very bossy and liked to order his women around. He asked her to get both a beer and a shot for him, and when she returned, he seemed to swallow the beer in one gulp, the shot with another, and then ordered her to get another round. She smiled at this, and just as a star is born in the galaxy, the relationship between them was then established.

I got good and drunk that night. After getting completely shitfaced and having a few words with another hockey player friend of mine, I walked the long way back to my dormitory, weaving and bobbing the whole way in my loneliness and my shame. I went to bed alone, thinking over and over how she should have been the one to get me that beer. Perhaps I would have had her in my bed by now.

When I woke up the next morning, I went to vomit in the bathroom and then slept for a few hours more. Back then, I could tolerate hangovers and sicknesses of this sort. If I did the same things now, I'd probably wind up in the hospital or at least in jail for a drunk and disorderly charge.

But in college, the beer always flowed, the cheapest and most disgusting beer available, and I actually started liking my drunkenness with brands of beer that were the worst of the lot. Schlitz, Lowenbrau, Meisterbrau, Milwaukee's Best, Natty Daddy. These were the beers that I imbibed. No wonder I wanted to vomit in the morning. But once I made it through my terrible hangovers, I was out there again, at the same fraternity parties, eyeing the women and hoping they would stop ignoring me.

I just didn't fit in, and maybe they hated that the most - my refusal to conform and my willingness to learn how to respect women regardless of how they actively ignored me. I don't think their disliking me was such a secret either. It had been known up to that point that women just didn't like me at all. Their ignoring of me had grown conspicuous. I'm still mystified by them, because I was the one they chose to ignore. I still can't figure out why. Instead, I hung out with my one ice hockey friend. While he talked to the women, I stood to the side - chugging beer, a shot every half-hour, and I had a penchant for staring at his women in all of their loveliness.

I stayed alone drunk on booze for quite some time at the college. And trust me, there were many students who were worse alcoholics there than I. I visited the fraternity house every week when they had weekday parties just to interrupt the college's academic atmosphere and replace it with both booze and even more comely women. I thought I was in heaven at that fraternity house. But that night, I was again ignored by a random sorority sister that I had the displeasure of meeting. She stood near the entrance way of the basement of the fraternity house where all of the partying took place. I introduced myself and then fired away with questions about her life.

"So, where are you from?" I asked.

"Virginia."

"Really? You're a long way from home."

"I know. But I'm here now, and I'm heading in the right direction."

"Good for you. What are you studying?"

"Economics."

"Good for you. That's an excellent major. How much time do you have to go to graduate?"

"A couple of years."

"Great! What do you think of the college?"

"It's fine."

I couldn't understand what made her so terse in her statements. She didn't smile but only winced, as though it pained her to lose focus on the fraternity and sorority mixer that night. She didn't smile once, and I actually thought that maybe I caused her some kind of social distress by asking her

7

these questions, no matter how ordinary or vapid these questions were.

The women at the college were very conscious of their social standing. It was often the case that the more beautiful the woman, the more popular she became, just so long as she joined the sorority to tap ancient witchcraft, surround herself with other hot women for protection, and find a similarly hot guy-friend who somehow infiltrated the sorority ranks with his coolness and charisma. It was quite a scene this way at the college. They might as well have chosen a prom queen as well. Like it really mattered at that age anyway.

We were becoming adults all of a sudden. Back then, we were definitely trying to be older, but this translated into the bad behavior of drinking a lot, having one-night stands, cheating on tests, wearing stuff from *Brooks Brothers*, and driving around in Reagan-era luxury sports cars.

And it wasn't like I cared, but most of the students I had known there were red, white, and blue Reaganite Republicans born with the promises of good character, wealth, the freedom not to be so taxed or regulated, the opening up of the world to keep the rat-race at a steady, global pace.

I fell in the middle of the road somewhere. It was safe this way, and whenever there was serious political talk, I abstained. I could only shrug my shoulders. The students there were smart. They were too smart, and like myself, they had been blessed with five-star educations, as their parents taught them about money and savings and getting a good job to take all of life's pain and misery away. They distilled life into a few basic instructions on what to do while working on a job for a few of the multinational insurance companies in downtown Hartford or the ceaseless trading that governed the New York Stock Exchange. Everyone wanted money. The students struggled with a purpose - to strike that right balance between having ordinary lives, but at least happy and prosperous enough to preserve that ordinariness.

Don't get me wrong. I respected them. In some cases, I even loved them. I had a drinking problem, academic concerns, girls who ignored me, just one friend, and I think that's all the food the Good Lord had put on my plate back then. I just couldn't talk it up like the others did.

I didn't know what to expect from these beauty-queen sorority sisters, but I had heard so many tales about how they let the ongoing suppression of sexuality linger and turn into poisonous knives aimed in my direction. These were stories about how such-and-such took a woman home that night and fucked her brains out, only for her to wind up in the fraternity rumor mill after they saw the girl's glazed eyes at the very next fraternity party. I went to those parties, but I never had a chance. I guess I was too much of an introvert for them to notice how I lurked in the shadows, stared at them, thought about how I could get one on my own without having to fight my way through the heavyweights who protected them.

Interestingly enough, there were many at that fine college who had to fight their way onto the social register to get anywhere with them. These were hopeless men. But they earned my sympathy, because with women there is little choice but to fight for them, or at least ruffle a few feathers in an attempt to cure a man's young lust. We could easily tell who the beautiful people were. I never looked to their insides. Personality didn't matter much. I concerned myself with their shapes, their bodies, their longing side-glances at the men they would sleep with night after night. It could have driven me insane, but even in the face of the intense New England beauty I wanted, I never knew how fierce the race for a mate could be. I didn't even try to chase one down. As they say, when the fire is too hot, get out of the kitchen. Every fraternity party turned into this - this pulsing, throbbing cauldron of hormones attempting to connect, when all I could really do is play the wallflower and gawk at these wealthy, beautiful women - the type that called Boston their capital city, whether or not they were Irish Catholic.

I was having a tough time of it, because these women were starting to give in - to what I'm not sure, but instead of seeing me as this Exeter nerd, they saw me more as a scholar-athlete. They liked what they saw, and a couple of weeks later after midterm exams, I returned to the same fraternity, and it was then that I met her. Her name was Sophia. She was a sorority sister out for a good time.

Like the last girl I met down in the bowels of the fraternity house, she seemed to reject me without saying a word. And Sophia's snobbery flared as she offered me her stuck-up, pointed nose and looked away as I tried to start a decent conversation with her. I thought it was cute - that this was another woman who wanted to defeat me and pummel me to the beer-soaked basement floor of the fraternity house could have easily cut me to shreds with her intelligence. The women always seemed smarter at playing these ridiculous games. She knew how to play, though, and just to have a chance to get through to her, I also played the game. I was already well on the hunt.

"Do you ever look at the people you talk to?" I asked.

"I look away when I don't want to be bothered," she said.

"So then why did you come down here, if you don't want to talk to anyone?"

"I just don't want to talk to you, which is why I'm looking away."

She smiled at her own comment, as though she had touched upon some kind of feminine genius that had repelled all sorts of students who wanted to get down her pants.

"Well, if you looked at the people you talked to, maybe you'd find someone who interests you."

"I really doubt that."

"It would help if you smiled every now and then too. Maybe you'd have a better time of it."

"Listen," she said, "I don't mean to be rude, but I just want to be left alone right now, which is why I'm looking away, okay? Why don't you go and pour yourself another beer?"

"How about I get you one?"

"I don't drink," she said. "I'm here for the mixer. And you're not a brother here. Why would I be interested in you?"

"Because I'm handsome."

"I don't think so."

"I'm smart."

"Probably not."

"And I have good taste in women."

"This is true, but you're wasting your time chasing them around. I know how you guys operate. You just want sex, just like every other man at this college. You see women as objects. The only way you like women is if they are good-looking. You really don't care about what we think or how we behave."

"That's just not true. I both respect and appreciate women. Isn't that what you want?"

"Yeah, but I doubt I'll get the respect I deserve from you."

"That's because you don't want to be respected by men. You like the drama of being abused, shit on, taken for your money, because those are the types of guys you're interested in."

"Where'd you get that theory from? Hustler Magazine?"

"Hey, that's a good magazine! They publish a lot of stuff on politics that no one ever reports. At least the magazine has balls."

"Oh, yeah," she said. "I forgot. Men like you read it for the expert reporting."

She did something remarkable again. She actually turned to face me. I could tell that such a debate could go on forever. She liked arguing about this topic - a battle of the sexes. She knew more than I did, as she probably majored in Women's Studies at the fair college. These types of women come to parties prepared. They feigned their academic prowess and their disassociation with men just to feel superior to men, whom, I guessed, were trash. Yet now that she actually faced me, I knew I had a chance.

"Let's talk about something else besides sexual politics, okay?" I wound up saying.

"Why? Because I won the argument?"

"Gloat if you want to, okay? And I like arguing with you. You're foolish not to go out with me, if I were to decide to ask you out."

"The answer is no," she smiled. "Not in a million years."

"I think you'd like a guy like me. You can win every argument, and I can become your slave for the Amazonian female community that you live with. They'll make you a commando."

She smiled again, and I could tell that I was making her laugh. And it didn't matter where I stood on gender politics. Women will always love a guy who makes them laugh. I was getting her closer to saying yes to me. She was probably the most beautiful woman at the fraternity house that night. And because of this she was aloof and didn't seek any sort of commonality or connection with anyone who wouldn't justify the excesses of her ego and erudition. I almost wanted to congratulate her for having the same level of ego as any man in the place. Yet, I didn't want to be critical with her at that mixer. Slowly, I was working it. I planted the seeds of a relationship.

She did smile a few times, but these little smiles that I dragged out of her were soon nullified as she snapped back into that same aloofness, that same inability to connect with anyone human but the rebellious books she must have read. Nevertheless, I at least made her smile.

"How about I get you a drink," I said.

"That's your answer to everything? A drink?"

"It helps with socializing. A beer might loosen us up."

"So you can get me in the sack at the end of the night?"

"No. It would just help you be more of a human being."

"For humanity's sake?"

"Something like that, yes."

"Well, you are kind of cute. You are a funny creature. You can get me one beer, but after that, I'm not drinking anymore. Half of the people who come out of these fraternities are alcoholics."

"I'm not a brother here."

"Just get me the beer, okay?"

I went to the bar right after I had cracked the door that opened up her world, and I got her a beer topped to the brim of a flimsy plastic cup. The brother working behind the taps also poured me the beer with no foam - just the clear, golden elixir that had always worked so well in getting me a little tipsier and more confident and adventurous. Gone were my crippling shyness and fear of approaching the type of woman who would immediately cut my heart out.

I brought the beers back to where she was, but she was gone. I had no idea where she ran off to. I looked for her several times down in that party-hardy basement, but she was nowhere to be found. I even asked around. No one knew where this Queen Bee had gone. Just when you warm these women up, they torture you by disappearing. I had no idea where she lived on campus. Hell, I didn't even know her name yet. I just had to hope that she would be at the next fraternity party.

There were several late-night gatherings at the Greek side of campus, and I knew that most of the sorority sisters of this caliber usually hung out at another fraternity a block or two away. Even though I didn't like doing it, I knew I would have to chase her around until her defenses and her shields blocking a marauding man grew weak and tired. I just had to open myself up and let her insult me. Let her have my ego. Let me be her slave and follow her around from now until the hereafter. Yes, I was willing to do anything to talk to her again. She would make my life much better, because I knew that her Daddy probably gave her a lot of money. We're talking full tuition and immediate sorority membership, paid in full.

I left that previous night with a vacancy at my chest. I felt that I had dug deeply within her and went where no other man had gone.

On my way home, my own personal walk of shame to my dormitory, I knew that I had to chase her around, and no, I did not have to submit to an interrogation, and I didn't have to reveal my income statements to get a woman like her. We were at a wealthy college after all, and that people were wealthy at the college had been tacitly known to all of us. Also, most people were white like myself, so there was that bonding of white men and women, a kind of ease with which whiteness lent us shared experiences without blacks or brown people getting in the way.

Sadly, we couldn't relate to those with diverse backgrounds. Relationships between men and women at the college only existed among those with the same skin color, as skin color was a sign that brought messages of what we all thought about the blacks and persons of color on campus and their lives of suffering, discrimination, and abject poverty. They were poor, and they dumped their waste out onto the streets where they lived.

I used to think that we were lucky as white people. Being in a relationship with a black woman would have added endless complications to the simple process of the chase. At the college, the two races remained separate.

17

Rarely did one find a fraternity party with a healthy mix of black and white people. We kept our distances as white students. The black students kept theirs.

I went to one of my classes the next morning. I remember now how easy it was to cope with hangovers. I awoke tired, but nowhere near to the wreckage of the harder, more bitter hangovers that confront me now. Back then, I could wake up early and easily make it to class without any headaches, heartburn, or nausea. Since we were young, we were allowed to have our fair share of beer or wine. Some smoked pot but not so much. Alcohol ruled the parties with the good-looking women, mainly because of its unwavering place in New England upper-class society. Cheap beer was at least legal, while pot or heroin or cocaine were not. The people on the hockey team had a distaste of street drugs. Most of the players in provincial fashion only dealt with alcohol. We stuck to fraternity parties, some tobacco smoking, and beer. I loved beer, and I still drink it today.

In class, though, no one participated in any of the discussions that the professor put out there. The class was quiet, and the professor's droning on about Western Civilization nearly put all of us to sleep. It had interested me, though, how these same types of women were in the class and said absolutely nothing. It occurred to me back then, that the good-looking college students were way too concerned with their image and social standing rather than learning anything of value. The men had this affliction as well, but I never expected the women to keep silent and wait until the most boring class on earth ended.

I recognized some of these women. They went to drink the night before, just like I did. None of them looked hungover. They were athletes, in a sense. They cared only about the game, just like Sophia cared. If they spoke up or reacted to any of the ideas advanced by the professor, it would put them at risk. They kept silent. Yes, they wrote their papers and handed them in on time, but they lacked the courage to speak in class. It seemed like I was the only one in the class making any effort at addressing what the professor asked, even if his ideas were ridiculous, or at least ridiculous on purpose, just to get an agree or disagree from the quiet women who simply sat and looked around the room at the fraternity brothers they had crushes on.

It never worked, though. The professor could have been a white supremacist, and they would have still remained quiet and calculating. They must have been planning for the next party or who to date, who to touch, and who to avoid like the plague. They disliked geeks, and as one of the sole participants in the class, I could again see why they hated me. They headed towards mating season, while I set my sights on high academic achievement. I knew I had to change my ways in order to land Sophia. I thought that maybe I should be quiet in the classroom too.

And yet, I had to respond to the professor's questions, because no one else would, and it was eerie in the cold silence when everyone there remained dead silent. My hand shot up, I participated, and then I felt embarrassed for advancing my point of view. I had a terrible time of it in that class. The hotter the women are in the classroom, the less likely they're going to behave academically. And now I was the geek responding to the professor. The dead calm of silence could have continued without my interjections, but I had to do something. Even the professor knew about the dreaded silence of the hot women in his class who were unable to develop their minds. They weren't shy at all outside of the classroom, but within it, they didn't say a word. It pissed me off a little bit too.

After class, the professor pulled me up to the front and said that he admired my ideas. All the women had left by then. They left as quickly as they came in. I was again the head geek.

I went to my dorm room, opened my mini-fridge, and had a few beers before the next fraternity party. I knew I'd find her at the other fraternity down the block, and the fraternity brothers there didn't exactly like me, but I knew that I had to go in there just to find her. I hated the idea of following her around. I didn't want her to think of me as some kind of perverted stalker. I just wanted another conversation at least to draw her in, to engage her fierce and protected enigmas like Nixon's opening up of China. So, I went, and I stood on a long line after dropping five bucks at the entrance.

A good reggae band played up front that night, and all around me were the prettiest women at the college. Some of the people there lit up joints, but I wanted nothing to do with drugs. These women were perfect-looking, while I moved up near the band away from them, mostly because I felt like a creep. Some of these sorority sisters from the night before even recognized me. They must have used their psychic powers to communicate to everyone within range that the weird creep who actually participated in class discussions had arrived. They looked at me and then turned away. Some of them gave me terrible looks and then rolled their eyes. But I wanted to find Sophia.

When I went up to the bar for my first drink of the night, I found her. She was at the tail end of the bar drinking shots provided by the fraternity brothers that surrounded her. She enjoyed herself. She smiled with them, getting totally shitfaced, and yet, I needed to disrupt them. I could have caused a fight if I didn't approach her with the utmost delicateness. I managed to move through the massive crowd of people at the bar and broke up the conversation she had. "How ya doin'!" I said to her.

I then did the unthinkable. I darted in for a kiss on her cheek. I can tell you now that her cheek was soft and warm, as though she constantly used skin lotion for her face. And then the fraternity guys got a little jumpy.

"Do you know this guy?" one of them asked.

I could have been ejected from the party for committing the crime of a kiss. One word from Sophia, and the fraternity brothers would have kicked me into the gutter.
This, however, did not turn out that way.

"It's okay," she said, smiling to them.

At least she was happy that night. She pulled me away from the bar to an uncluttered area of the fraternity.

"What the hell do you think you're doing?" she asked.

"Sorry," I said. "I guess my lips just wandered to your face. I couldn't help it."

"You actually kissed me. I should let my friends kill you."

"And you have that power. Why, then, do I think you liked it?" "Don't make me get one of my friends over here. You had no right to kiss me."

"I had to. You're the reason why I came here. I wanted to talk to you. Maybe we should get to know each other a little more."

And then she said, "do you know what we did before the party tonight?"

"You mean here?"

"Yes, here. We did a few lines of coke on a mirror at the bar, and we were also drinking happily until you arrived. I knew from last night that you'd be such a bummer."

"So, you're on coke right now?"

"Yeah. And you can't even afford talking to my dealer."

"Coke is not good. You can easily become addicted to that stuff."

"Oh, so now you're my father, eh? Trying to tell me how to run my own life?"

"I'm here, because I don't want you to ruin it."

"Let's make a deal, then," she said. "If I give you a kiss on the cheek, like you gave me, you'll never talk to me again? Does that sound like a good deal?"

"I'll have to think about it. Hey, though, do want another beer?"

"Don't try to change the subject," she said. "So, do you want to kiss me on the cheek? I'll only do it if you want me to do it."

"I do want you to do it."

I finished my cup of beer and then stood with her as the reggae band played on, the party getting slammed with people who were rushing into the place. Everyone seemed jovial and very drunk, except for Sophia, now that she had to kiss me. After deliberating on it, I made the deal. But when she leaned her lips in to kiss my cheek, I immediately turned my cheek and kissed her mouth.

I had to do it. I just had to, because I wanted her. I wanted her more than her coke-snorting fraternity friends or her stuck-up sorority sisters. I had to let her know. She appeared stunned, as though the kiss on her lips was somehow a violation of her inner-core. I waited for her to respond, but she couldn't. She simply pursed her lips, returned to the bar away from where I stood, and did a shot with her gathering of friends.

I had little idea of what her friends said to her, but a couple of them went upstairs to the living quarters of the fraternity house. She followed them, I guess, to do some more coke and to spare herself from anything remotely romantic. I could tell that the kiss rocked her world, but I didn't know what would happen next.

After a few more beers, I left the party and returned to my dorm room. I pulled out another beer from my minifridge and also drank heavily from a top-shelf bottle of whisky I had saved for really fucked up occasions. I couldn't stop thinking about kissing her, replaying the event in my

mind. She knew I meant business. Nothing could dare
reverse that kiss.

But on the next night, I went to the fraternity I had been
used to, and in a very mild and even discrete manner, I
celebrated, because I knew that she thought about the kiss I
gave her, making her beautiful mind revolve around that
totally unsolicited anomaly. This was the type of woman
whom no one messed with, I had to remember that. Even
something so simple as a kiss, and in this case, a surprise
kiss, ruffled her peacock feathers. She would want revenge,
but I'm not sure what form it would take.

When she came down the fraternity steps to the bar area,
I tried to hide from her. First, I wanted to judge her mood
and her demeanor that night. If she looked pissed, then I had
to leave, even though I could have watched her near the bar
for hours with the two bookends she brought with her from
the other fraternity house with her. The guy pouring the beer
knew these people, and they shook hands. After pouring
them a second, I saw the bartender's hand point towards me,
as I lurked in the shadows waiting for an appropriate
response. By the time the two bookends of hers walked over
to where I stood, I bolted from the fraternity house and ran
for my very life. I looked over my shoulder and saw that her
two men were definitely after me. I was filled with booze, so
I couldn't run very fast. One of them grabbed my shoulder

from behind and pulled me to the ground on the nearby football field. I knew it was over.

They held me by the collar. Through their heavy breathing, I could hear them grunt and mutter a few choice curse words, as they held me down. I then saw Sophia running after them. I could see her leave from the fraternity house steps. She then slowed and walked casually to where we were. When she got there, her two toughs popped me in the face a couple of times. One of the bookends again pinned me down to the ground by trapping me with his boot to my chest. I bled from the corner of my mouth, and I could feel a welt gather on my cheek.

After she arrived and looked down upon me, her abundant chest heaving, she told the toughs to return to their own fraternity, but not without their saying, "you asshole, if you ever step foot near her again, we're going to do some serious damage. Stay away from her."

The one who had pinned me down released his boot, and both returned to their own fraternity up the block, leaving me sprawled out on the sidewalk by the classrooms. So suddenly, I was alone with Sophia. She looked angry, but she would not return to the other fraternity where her two buddies went. She simply looked down at me and said, "So why did you kiss me that way?"

"I don't know," I whined in pain. "I like you, that's probably why."

"In other words, you violated the boundaries of a woman just because you like her? Doesn't it matter what the woman wants too?"

"I'm sorry, but I had to do it. I had no choice."

"Of course, you had a choice. Couldn't you have tried starting a decent conversation?"

"I tried that. It didn't work."

She continued to stand over me as warm blood filled my mouth.

"And do you know," she said, "that it creates a lot of bad stress when you say that you like me? You shouldn't say that to a woman. Any woman."

"Again," I said, as my normal breathing returned, "I really like you, and one of these days, you're gonna like me too. And I'm going to make you mine."

She didn't respond to my line of reasoning. She simply said,

"get up. Just get up."

It was difficult, but I lifted my drunk and defeated body from the football field. I stumbled a little. Finally, I stood up straight and looked her in the eyes.

"So now what?" I asked. "Are you going to beat me up a second time if I say that I like you?"

She moved closer to me, kissed my cracked lips and ran the soft well of her palm down my bruised face.

"Men are such fools," she said calmly, as though she were used to having her tough guys kick the shit out the men who wanted her.

"I'll be at the other fraternity up the block tomorrow night.

That's where I usually hang out. You can meet me there." she said.

"But how can I go in there now? They'll beat me up."

"I'll take care of that. Now go home and put some ice on your face."

"Yes, ma'am. I'll see you tomorrow night then."

"Maybe you will," she said, "or maybe you won't."

"Then I'll have to search for you."

"Better not look too hard. Those two guys like beating up people like you."

I limped my way home, and when I spit on the sidewalk of the long journey to the other side of the campus, I spit blood. I didn't think anything of it, though. There was probably a cut somewhere in my mouth. Those guys really knew how to kick the shit out of people. They might as well have been bouncers for the exclusive night clubs in downtown Hartford, not that Hartford was much of an exclusive town at the time anyway. I resolved, though, that I would go in and search for her at her fraternity hangout the next night. Until then, I finally arrived home, washed my mouth out with beer, and had a couple more, and even a cold one for my cheek. Even though her protectors beat me up, she at least kissed me and held her hand to my bruised face. I had gotten through to her, and even though I would have to be really cautious about any long silences, I rehearsed my imaginary conversations with her in the mirror that night and then passed out on my messy bed at dawn.

On the next day, I didn't participate in class, which caused the professor to call me up to his desk afterwards. He was a nice man, well-educated, and tremendously smart, but also incredibly boring.

His hoary beard and tweed suit placed his niceness first and his amazing intelligence second. He reminded me of Santa Claus.

"Hi, Charlie," he said, "how's everything going?"

"Fine, Professor. Things are going well."

"I can see that you got beaten up."

"Yeah. I got into an altercation at one of the fraternities. It's no big deal. I'm healing up nicely."

He scratched his beard for a moment and said, "you didn't say much of anything during the class, Charlie. It has me concerned. Are your bruises the reason why you didn't participate today?"

"I just don't want to bring any attention to myself."

"Charlie, I don't need to tell you that you are one of the top students in this class. Hell, you're one of the only ones who says anything."

"I know, Professor."

"I know this college can be a tough place socially. I hope that you still stick to academic achievement. The graduate schools like to see good grades too. You shouldn't be sucked in by the social environment. It will take your achievements away.

"I'm just getting to learn that," I smiled.

"Well, Charlie, you can always come to me. You know that, right?"

"Yes, sir, I do. Thank you, Professor. I'm glad that you care." "Enjoy the weekend, then, and stay out of trouble is what I would advise. But by Monday, I expect to see your old self come to class and not just another student who hides in the back."

"Yes, Professor. I should be back on track after the weekend. Sorry if I caused any concern."

He was a good man, or rather, he was good to me that afternoon. Granted that I didn't know much about him other than what I saw in class, but I could tell that he had a lot of integrity surrounding that snowy, wizened hair of his. He had been at the college for thirty years. If only others in the class participated more, but they usually ran the risk of being stigmatized for bringing up academics within the fraternity/sorority party loop.

I still maintained my independence as a student, though. I wanted to learn. There was no loss, since I already met the woman of my dreams the night before. And now she wanted to hang out with me at the other fraternity. I couldn't have been happier. My day of classes was eclipsed by wild imaginings of having conversations with her, pillow talking, dressing up for special events, and even having children. While these were all fantasies of mine, I did think that I had a shot, even though she was way out of my league.

I took a quick nap after classes that morning. The short power nap helped me tremendously, because now I was ready for a night with Sophia. I didn't know what to expect, only that I would have quite a hangover the next day, but who was looking so far into the future? I had to keep things within the *now*. And the now looked good so far.

After dinner, I made preparations. I finally put on an oxford shirt, tan chinos, and a sweater. I was accepted all of a sudden. I checked myself in the mirror several times. Once I was ready and the sun had set, I walked out on fraternity row under the heavy clouds of night. Music filled the rarefied air as the nighttime parties were just beginning. I walked to the other fraternity house where she hung out. I saw her with a couple of her guy friends at the bar drinking a beer. How I loved beer back then. She was a woman I could drink with, which turned me on even more. Even though she had all-natural beauty, she was still down-to-earth enough to drink mass quantities of terrible beer. She gulped her beer down, and her two bookends made sure that she received another one whenever she wished. Here was a woman with clout.

I didn't want to walk up to her right away, especially with her protectors surrounding her. I walked up to a part of the long bar that was densely packed with revelers, and I ordered my beer there. I made sure to milk my beer, because I didn't want her to see me just yet. I needed courage, because she must have always surrounded herself with the antagonistic forces that repelled guys like me. Also, I wanted to hoist my courage up, and the beer usually did that for me.

I waited for several minutes wondering when I'd catch her alone. The overhead music began to spew out popular rock tunes, and after only ten minutes, the fraternity zoomed ahead in getting as many people to the bar as possible. The women were let in for free, while the men had to pay the cover charges.

I was on my third beer when I walked to where she sat at the other side of the bar. She seemed to be having a good time. She sung some of the tunes that were on the overhead speakers. She looked fantastic, and I hate to be so stuck on one feature of a woman, as women are usually multidimensional and have many qualities, but Sophia looked as beautiful as the night before, and the few beers that I had at the bar only enhanced her beauty. I walked up to her nervously, hoping that she would take the lead. But with women these days, no one can really tell what they find appropriate.

Modern society had little choice but to make women the choosers of their own mates, while men could only do so much to win their own. One could easily get jail time if one didn't approach a woman in the right way these days. All the power had been given to them, while men could only fight over these women, as though it were a Mr. America contest, a fierce competition to give the women a broad spectrum of guys, and she would pick the one she wanted to be with. No longer could the man make the first move. These women had to, and they would wait until their top choice presented himself, like cattle at an auction.

She smiled when I walked closer to her. She spotted me, and again I felt a little nervous. I wanted our conversation to go smoothly, as though it were scripted for television. The place smelled of stale beer, and it became loud and rowdy after sometime.

I leaned over to her ear, and introduced myself again.

33

"You made it," she said.

"Yeah. I came all the way here to talk to you."

"I take it you are from the other side of campus?"

"Yeah. I had to walk there last night after we had our episode."

"There are a lot of geeks on the other side of campus," she said.

"That's why I live on this side."

"It's fraternity row, really."

"Yes. I like this fraternity the most. They know how to treat women."

"Apparently, you have very big friends."

"They protect me from guys like you, especially the geeks who think their minds can do all the work to get me and nothing else. But you? I kind of like you. You really threw me for a loop last night."

"I couldn't help it."

"Why don't we go upstairs. There's too much noise down here."

"Am I allowed to go up?"

"If you're with me, there's no problem."

"I guess, I'm with you then," I said, nervously.

The upstairs of this fraternity house had soft couches, recliner chairs, and a couple of highly expensive Persian rugs. A separate bar in the back of the room served members of the fraternity and their guests. At this time, though, most of the brothers were downstairs, hitting on the women. I had Sophia, and I casually walked over to the empty bar and poured us some more beer. Sophia didn't seem to be bothered by this. I could take custody of the keg without a problem, as though I myself was a fraternity brother there. She actually smiled. I must have looked too clumsy working the taps.

She then sat down on one of the couches. In front of the couch was a large coffee table with drawers on its sides. After I settled down with Sophia on the couch, I noticed how quickly Sophia pulled open one of the drawers in the coffee table to collect what she must have left there the night before. She took out a mirror and a small pouch of a white powder.

"Interested?" she asked.

"No, but thanks."

"God, I hope you're not the boring type. Beer and pot get old after a while, wouldn't you say?"

"I like the old-fashioned way - just beer, and maybe a joint on occasion."

"So, I take it you've never tried this?"

"No. I try to stay away from hard drugs."

"This is hardly a hard drug. I just use it to have a little fun. Do you want to try it? It will give the evening a little lift."

I knew it might lead to that, so I declined, even though I wanted nothing more than to be closer to her in the private space of the fraternity that evening. She did the line as tough she was experienced in using the drug, and right after she snorted it up her beautiful nostril, she became ebullient and alive. She smiled for once.

"What do you want to do now?" I asked.

"How about we go up to the third floor? There's a bedroom upstairs. We can talk at least without hearing all of the music from downstairs."

I followed her up a rickety, wooden staircase, and I made sure not to make any moves once we were in the new room we found ourselves in. I put that responsibility on her shoulders. I didn't want her to throw me out for being too eager. But when she took off her clothes and revealed herself to me, I must have immediately fallen in love - not necessarily with her intelligence or personality - but with the aesthetic and lush naturalness of her body.

She was an Anglo-American just like me, and I wanted to touch her right away. I had traveled eons to be with such a woman, and she fell asleep in my arms after her high from the coke wore off. She was great in bed, and from that point, I knew that she was the one. There was little doubt in my mind that the angels sent had down a beautiful gift that night.

36

We fell asleep in each other's arms. I woke up early the next morning on the third floor of the fraternity to find her gone.

So suddenly I found myself in what seemed to be the foreign territories of her unfriendly, upstairs fraternity. I heard the music downstairs. It must have been four or five in the morning, and the party still raged on without interruption. I put on my clothes, and searched for her downstairs. After looking over every corner and crevice of the basement party room, I knew she wasn't there anymore. I figured she must have gone back to her dorm, which, in any case, was on the same block as fraternity row. I walked myself home after that to the other side of the campus.

I kept seeing Sophia most often at the other fraternity. I became a quick convert from the fraternity to which I had usually gone to the one where she drank and hung out with her fellow sorority sisters. There were a few men there too, mostly the brothers who eyed me suspiciously and wondered why I was there and not elsewhere. Sophia cleared it up with them, and she basically invited me to visit her every night. She drank hard, and when she summoned me upstairs, she didn't care at all that I passed on all of her attempts to use the cocaine. It seemed that a lot of her sisters were also on the drug, and that gave their sorority a common bond. They all used and seemed to have a good time using it.

She said she did cocaine recreationally, but from what I saw, she was doing it almost every night. We started sleeping together in the third-floor bedroom of that fraternity house, but I didn't want to sleep with her all the time, even though the sex was good. I wanted her to her like me - not the side of me that drank a lot, or her side that did coke most of the time. It was almost as though I wanted to keep our relationship Platonic, because I fell fast for her, and I didn't really know how to approach her, now that I could see a pattern of addiction commencing. I wanted to see what she was like outside of these fraternities.

I did ask around though, and, apparently, she did well academically. She just didn't talk about it much, as though the rest of the college was another world to her that she dealt with in her own way. She never liked mixing business with pleasure. They stood far apart. After all, we were there to study and not just to party all the time.

"I don't think we should do this anymore," I said to her on the third floor, after our usual love-making session.

"Do what?"

"Sleep together. I don't think it's a good idea. I hardly know anything about you."

"Well, what do you want to know?"

"Tell me about your family."

"They live in the Boston area right now. My parents are actually divorced, and I have a younger brother who goes to school up there."

"Whereabouts?"

"He'll be graduating from Roxbury Latin in June."

"Must be a smart kid."

"Yeah, he is, but I'm smarter than he is, though," she smiled.

"What do your parents do?"

"I don't want you to meet my parents just yet, if that's where this line of questioning is going."

"I don't think I should meet them yet, no, but I just wanted to know more about them too."

"My father runs an investment firm," she said, "and my mother is a homemaker. Anything else?"

"I guess that's it for now. Hey, how about we have dinner in

Hartford tonight. My treat."

"Hartford? Yuck. I don't want to get mugged or raped."

"Don't be silly. Hartford is a great town. There's a lot to do. It just so happens that this college is in a tough neighborhood is all. All of Hartford isn't that way."

"Well, we have another party here tonight."

"But that's late night. I'm talking about dinner time."

"Just go home for now."

"How about you take me to your place?"

"I don't want to wake my roommates up."

I could tell that she wasn't very interested in telling me more, which made me wonder where this flimsy relationship of ours headed. I needed more - not just her beauty or seeing her at parties, but I needed more, and she wouldn't pull the barricades off the door and let me in. It became frustrating seeing her night after night. She did say that she liked sleeping with me, but that's about it, and I wondered how I would move our relationship forward, now that I had been sleeping with the most beautiful woman on campus.

For some reason, everyone wanted this woman, as though her beauty gave everyone around her good luck. But I wanted to take a break, because I wanted to be sure that she liked me. Hell, maybe she could find a way to love me too? I guess I just wanted more and more of her - to reveal the scars she must have hidden, to know the places she loved, even the type of guys she liked, because for some strange reason, she didn't want the relationship to grow. She wanted to keep it at the same level, as though she micro-managed me to some extent and kept her secrets hidden down so deeply that no one could find them, not even a person who shared intimacy with her. It became a frustrating task. I had to know if, underneath her behavior, she felt the same way I felt about her. I asked her this up on the third floor while stroking her blonde locks in bed.

"Do you see our future?" I asked.

"I don't look too far ahead," she said.

"I just seem to want more and more of you. Do you know what that's like?"

"Not really, no," she said.

"It's something akin to torture."

"I'm sorry. Am I torturing you by being in bed with you so often? Maybe we should see less of each other."

"That would kill me," I said.

I continued to stroke her hair, kissing her intermittently on her cheek. I had already fallen for this woman. I feared it was too late. I rushed in, and I couldn't help but feel a little lost, because I didn't know what I was doing anymore.

Over the past few weeks, my grades had slipped. My professor in Western Civilization continued to be concerned, until I told him that a woman was doing this to me.

"Some things are more important than academia," he said, scratching his beard. "Some things are more important than grades.

Do you like this woman?"

"I think this could be the one, Professor."

"When two people are in love, the rules don't apply. I think it was from a song that I heard on the radio the other day. I couldn't help but thinking how true that is. And now my best student has been pulled in. I can only say that grades are not as important as the ways of love. Just ask my wife. She would agree."

"I like this woman, Professor."

"I know you do, Charlie. I know you do."

During that whole month, I had been seeing her nightly. We would get drunk, do a little coke, and stay in bed all evening She was an unofficial member of that fraternity, and while I tried to get her to return to my dorm room for a change, she didn't want to. She wanted to be near both the endless supply of beer and the white lines she snorted up with a silver straw. We grew comfortable just lying together. We didn't necessarily need to have sex. Just cuddling did the trick. But when we did do it, it was close to magical. This was the woman I wanted to be my wife. But when she phoned me the next afternoon, she said she needed to see me. So, I obliged. We met in the main cafeteria in the Student Center. She looked distraught.

"Thanks for meeting me here," she said. She ate from a bowl of granola mixed in with a red, tangy yogurt.

"What's wrong, sweetie," I asked.

I was genuinely concerned. I hoped she wouldn't break up with me. Maybe we went too far in the short time we were together.

"Charlie," she said, "something happened."

"What is it, sweetie? You know you can tell me anything."

She rested her hand on my cheek, and said, "Charlie, I'm pregnant."

I was shocked by this revelation, but in another, more intimate way. I was also happy and satisfied that our relationship had grown to share the child that now grew within her.

"Are you sure?" I asked.

"I'm late."

"But I thought you were on the pill."

"I thought so too. Something must have gone wrong. Maybe I was too tired of taking it?"

We sat in silence for a time. I then ran my hand through her hair. Apparently, she struggled with the idea of having a child so early in her life. I knew that she wanted to wait until she had a good career. She wanted to travel the world, only for that to be taken away with the prospects of having a child to take care of.

"You actually look pleased by this," she said.

"I am pleased," I said. "I'm scared to death, but I am pleased. You're the one."

"Don't say that, Charlie. I'm too young to have a child."

43

"I don't think so. Motherhood usually happens to young women, isn't that the case?"

"Charlie, I want to end the pregnancy."

"Come again?"

"You heard me, Charlie. I don't want to repeat it, but I want to get an abortion. I'm not ready to have children."

"But we're in love, aren't we?"

"You're in love with me. I'm not so in love with you - not enough to have a child with you anyway."

"Sophia, we have to think about this some more, okay? I want to have your child. I love everything about you. I can take care of you. My family has enough to fund us. We can live in New Hampshire, if you like. Everything will be taken care of by my family and yours. Don't you see? We're blessed with this child. You may not want it now, but you'll regret it in the future, I know you will. We belong together, you and me."

"I'm sorry, Charlie, but I just don't feel like you do. My family can also take care of us, but what kind of child will we have? A child addicted to cocaine and cigarettes and booze? I can't have that, and neither will my family. I won't be surprised if they disown for me for all of the trouble I've caused them already. I'm sorry, Charlie, but it's my decision. I have to have an abortion, and as far as you and I are concerned, we're over."

"Think about what you're saying. That child will be a beautiful child, raised by two great, successful families. It won't be bad at all."

"I don't want to marry you, Charlie, and I don't want this child. I get to decide. Not you. I'm going to the clinic in Hartford tomorrow. It's already taken care of. All you do right now is walk away. Just walk away from me and don't turn back. Don't be a fool. We will never be able to raise this child, and I just don't want it, and I don't want you."

"I don't care if you don't want me," I said, "but the child too? Honey, we should have it."

"No!"

And then she bolted for the doors of the Student Center, forever away from my life.

I knew it was her decision, but what about my rights? I called a lawyer in town. It was very cut and dry, said the lawyer. A mother carries the weight of the pregnancy and is, therefore, favored in this situation. She can terminate the pregnancy without the father's consent. The Supreme Court had ruled it in *Planned Parenthood v. Danforth*. The woman has a right to her medical privacy, as the woman is more affected by the pregnancy.

There was very little I could do. From what a few of my fellow ice hockey players told me a few days later, she did get the abortion at the women's clinic in town.

Apparently, I was the last one to know. Everywhere I went, people somehow knew of it. I could only shed a tear every now and then, especially when I abandoned my course work at the college.

I was so demoralized by her decision that I didn't feel like studying anything anymore. I had this vision of having a perfect family with her, the two cars, the grand house in an exclusive neighborhood, dinner parties, nice clothes for the kids, but she just didn't feel that way. I was so distraught by it, that I withdrew from the college before graduation, hoping that I would someday return, but I never did intend on returning. Even my friend, the Professor, after telling him what had happened with a cup of coffee in his hand at the Faculty Club, agreed that I should take some time off, get over what had happened, and return to school once it flushed through my system.

But I never did return to the college so soon after that.

I had had such beautiful dreams, such visions. The beauty of those dreams was dashed for the reality of being without an education in a world gone mad with unfairness. Sometimes, we just have to admit that we have no control over what happens in our lives, that instead of the heroic stances we take against adversity, we are more or less ruled by such adversities as they happen to us, like a boxer absorbing punches without having the ability to hit back. My ambivalence and passivity soon became an integral part of me that I never wanted but had to accept. I became a ghost, waiting for things to happen, and discovering that they never did, no matter how much I tried to better my own life and forget about Sophia and the child that could have been. It became a life of crisis and my reactions to crisis. It ruled over my existence.

My father agreed with my mother that it would be better if I came home to New Hampshire to live for a little while, especially considering what had just happened. My parents cheered me up by paying for everything and putting me back on an appropriately-sized allowance, and yet I knew that staying with them couldn't have lasted very long. I felt like a kid again. I had to shovel snow, wash dishes, clean the place up whenever it needed it. I must have stayed there for a couple of months before a few interesting ideas found me.

It didn't involve returning to Trinity at all. It involved heading off to a big city someplace and getting a good job. Without a degree this would be tough, and my parents urged me to return to college, but I just wasn't feeling it. I didn't want to study anymore.

I kept on thinking how it was supposed to be, and how I could have easily married Sophia. It was my first lesson in the belief that God laughs at plans. Whatever was my fate had to be my fate. The stars didn't readjust for someone like me. I was alone until bothered or annoyed by something I didn't like, but even then, I buried it by taking plenty of punches to the gut, swallowing hard, and then moving on my dreary way.

Chapter Two

Living in Boston was an option, but the rents were very high as well as the exorbitant costs of living. So was New York. Places that used to be so cheap ten or twenty years ago had now grown terribly expensive, and the rents there were pricey unless one could find a good job or have an apartment on a train line to get you into the big city for work every morning.

New Jersey produced the same results - expensive by its proximity to the big city to the East, over-populated, and a public transportation system that hadn't witnessed change in years. Jersey was out as well. The only other place that I could remotely afford was Albany, New York.

With my family's help and understanding of the great weight that the mother of my aborted child put upon me those few months after dropping out of college, I arrived in Albany after a dreadfully cold winter of New Hampshire living. After a couple weeks of searching, I found a low wage gig recycling material for a scrap metal company near the Port of Albany, where all of the shipping vessels docked and unloaded their cargo. The job was to respond to people in Albany who needed their junk removed and recycled for resale.

Once we had the junk, we then broke it apart, salvaged the valuable materials, like steel and copper, and then sold

49

these metals back to industry. The company gave me an old truck to collect the junk and return it to the junkyard near the docks.

It's my theory that no job in America is ever easy. Even collecting junk, having the company truck, and getting to drive all over the city unsupervised wasn't so easy when I considered the weight of the junk I had to haul away - a lot of appliances, gutted cars and their rusted parts, old air conditioners and old cooling systems from an uneven past of intense summer heat. All of these items could be stripped down to their essential elements, hauled back to the junkyard, and bought by developers, construction workers, and other types of builders.

Even though the job was simple enough, my body wasn't ready for the heavy lifting. It was something I had to get used to, like exercise or physical conditioning. Instead of my mind working, my body had to work, and I became somewhat obsessive about those who have to lift heavy objects for a living, like movers or package handlers or landscapers. My body was too weak at first, and I was also a little regretful that I didn't take the advice of my father and finish up college before launching into the world.

Because I never finished up college, the thick glass ceiling hovering above my head shrunk me down to half of what I could have earned, had I stayed and graduated.

It was all over now, though. Even though I started to hate the hauling of heavy items to the back of my truck, it was what I had at the moment, and it would have been foolish to give it up. While I never drifted into complacency with hauling junk, it turned into a full-time job, as the difficulty became the lifting of cargo. Yet, I didn't want to lose all that I had learned at the college either. I had to find some way to exercise my mind, but, by the time I returned to my messy studio apartment in the 'hood, I could do no more but crash on my sofa after devouring a pint of Ben & Jerry's ice cream. I would turn on the television and vegetate in front of it for a couple of hours, and I usually crashed before the ten o'clock news. I was up again at five ayem every morning for more of this back-breaking work.

It became such a problem that I had to reach out to my parents again. The boss at the junkyard gave me a couple of days off, and even though I was on a bus back to New Hampshire, I felt like running there instead. One the way, the bus' wheels transformed into the legs of a running man along the highway. I didn't want to return to Albany, but my parents, being staunch advocates of money and working hard to get it, wouldn't let me stay beyond my two-day release.

During a more traditional sit-down meal of turkey and lots of stuffing, they basically said, "you can't stay here. We can't support you anymore. I will send you some emergency

51

money that you request every month, but that's the limit. You have your own life to lead now, and you are no longer a child. Your money is your money. Our money is our money."

And God, did my parents live well compared to what I had to live with back in Albany. At that dinner, my father basically gave me the terms of adulthood, despite what had happened at the college and even though I hadn't fully healed from that wound yet.

At dessert, a slice of homemade cheesecake with robust coffee, my father said, "you are on your own, Charlie. You have to make a life from this narrow, stupid, and unkind world. I am confident that you won't need us anymore after a time. You have to make a future with the cards that you have been dealt. Your mother and I can advise you on certain things, but you will get no more money from us. You have to learn how to be on your own."

"Dad, but this is my first time back in New Hampshire in a while.

Can't I get a break somewhere?" "As far as money is concerned?"

"Yeah."

"The answer is no. You pick yourself up by your bootstraps, get back in there, and do your job. If you don't like your job, you best find another one. We have provided everything for you, and I know that you are only twenty-one, but you have to work to make it. You have to deal with the unfairness, the work load, all of those things that no one likes. But you will get used to it, and at times, I am sure you'll flourish, but for now, I'll take you to the bus station tomorrow morning."

I didn't sleep well that night. I had the junk yard job on my mind the whole time. It was almost as though I feared going into work after my two-day weekend off. I wanted liquor and beer, just like the college I had gone to, but for some reason, I knew that college had officially ended. There was a whole, other plane of reality that I had missed - yes, the ordinary world, the dryness of that ordinary world, where people got old and perished due to its spectacular ordinariness. It became a cross between ordinary comforts and extraordinary dreams that no one in their right mind could reach. It remained almost a state of bored sophistication, this urbanity, that never really worked for any lonely creature. Even for those with plenty of friends, the world just had to appear like a shiny red apple in its newness and tradition within that same sense of newness for anyone to live. It had to be forever changing but always leading to the hedonism that hid under most of the clandestine impulses of man.

As the older one got, even these desires and impulses fade amid the need to have a righteous soul on the highway to the afterlife. And suddenly, I began to see my existence in very ordinary terms. Without my parents' direct help of funding my dreams of one day having a family, even though Sophia was the real cause of that curse, there would be no family.

I would never be able to comprehend how I would be able to take care of a family. I was poor. Sure enough, I saw life as a series of nightmares. This was also true. It would have been unconscionable of me to have a child. I just wasn't ready, and I mistakenly thought that Sophia had seen through that, even though I believed that I would get family support had there been a child. But there was no child, and there was never going to be one either. Sophia simply slipped through me. I wanted to contact her to smooth things over, but the college wouldn't give out that information in order to protect her privacy. Sophia was gone.

I woke up in the early morning of a Monday, and after a brief bowl of cereal, I dragged myself to the bus station and took the Greyhound back to Albany. It was still dark out, and my retired parents were still asleep before I left. I wouldn't call what they did treacherous at all. I was hurt more by the practicality of not being able to move forward without them, as the future only held laborious, hardscrabble employment for me. I knew that I had to learn of the world, armed only with my body this early in the game, but also having my mind on reserve in case other opportunities would help me limping back to Hartford from where I now lived in the Albany 'hood.

It would take time to get to know people in Albany. I knew that. Also, I had to remind myself that I chose Albany for its lower cost of living and not to make friends or find a Wonder Woman who would marry me right away. I may have looked elegant, as my parents had that look of elegance to them. But on paper, I made barely above minimum wage, and the future of having just enough money to pay the bills loomed large. And I lived in one of Albany's most violent and poorest sections. There was little way I could pull along any college education in Albany. I had to learn practical street knowledge or perhaps even to venture to a vocational school to find out how to use my hands and not my whole damned body, which never stopped paining. My head was shrinking too. Money had to be made.

When I returned to hauling junk back to the docks, my boss paired me up with a young black guy named Cash. Of course, Cash wasn't his real name. It was Cassius. While I knew Cassius to be an old slave name, I thought Cash did a better job of representing him. But I protested the move to have Cash as my trainee. He could have easily replaced me, and since I was training him, it almost seemed like the junkyard would drop me and let a cheaper-paid Cash take over my position. I didn't want that, as I still needed the job, and I had already psyched myself up for the hard labor market.

But Cash seemed like an easy-going guy, and he was also a few years younger than I. He never finished college either, but he had studied hard at Albany High School and came away with enough knowledge anyway. Actually, he looked like a drug dealer, but I had been confused by the idea that all of Albany's black young adults would go into the drug trade. Some of this was true, because no one could live on the low wages being offered by the jobs Albany offered to its uneducated.

Drug dealing was the life that most of these young men would take on, unless something drastic was done about it. And I loved the idea of a living wage, but this just wasn't going to happen. Maybe there would be a rise in the minimum wage, but as far as living off of the job went, hell, I would have wanted to be a genius drug lord too.

There were very few options - pay the colleges and universities for a degree over time, get additional income by being poor at the generous social services offices, or just join the dangerous drug trade and make thousands per week.

Now I call that a rough economy! And, no, I didn't want to wind up in jail. The only option that both of us had was hauling junk, and that's all I really cared about.

Cash had dreams, though. He dreamed big, and while I admired him for that, I also was sophisticated enough to realize that dreams are total bullshit. One just had to accept one's station in life. Cash just hadn't crossed that line yet, and I wasn't going to push him over that line either. He was younger, and he wanted to go places.

Cash, who sat in the passenger seat after a couple of weeks of training, did seem like a good-natured person. We actually became friends while hauling away all of that junk. He was a hard worker, but he never lost sight of the prize.

"Take a look," he said to me one afternoon.

He held out his smart phone, and it showed a map of some islands.

"Jamaica?" I asked.

"Nope, this is Fiji."

"Fiji? That's a country people know exists but never know where it actually is."

"Fiji is a group of islands in the South Pacific."

"Okay. What about Fiji?"

"That's where I want to go."

"They'll give you some vacation time when you build up to a certain number of hours. You'll get to Fiji."

"I don't think you understand," said Cash. "I want to live there for a while."

"For God's sake, why? There doesn't seem like there's much going on in Fiji."

"They have women."

"And?"

"I'm going to sow my seeds in Fiji."

"What?"

"You heard me right. As soon as I can get some money together, that's where I'm headed, and once there I'll put myself out to stud."

"And these women-islanders will make all the stops for you, is that right?"

"It's been done many times before - to start a new breed of people, to raise an army from fathering a family. It would only make these people stronger and loyal to me."

I thought this idea a little ridiculous, because I thought that Cash was too poor to handle the flight and the costs of living in Fiji. If he worked a straight year, maybe he would be able to afford a trip like that.

"You interested in coming?" he asked.

"Who? Me?"

"Hell, yes, you? I'm gathering the funds up right now.

All we need is a round trip ticket, which is the biggest expense. But once we get there, all we need is a little cash for room and board, and we have to pay the women."

"Seriously?"

"I'm serious. This is not a joke. It's serious. We get there, we stay a week, and in that week, we impregnate as many women as possible. It's a great idea, isn't it?"

"I don't know. I'd feel a little weird never knowing who my children were."

"But that's the thing. They are all your children, and they are on one, isolated island where no one gets into trouble."

"You better check it out," I said, "but isn't there, like, Hurricanes and Cyclones there and stuff?"

"Every now and then. It is, after all, an island in the middle of nowhere. The place has problems just like any other place. But I guess what I'm doing is fulfilling my dreams. Just like the Pharaohs of Egypt. I have to impregnate as many women as possible. And then, maybe after I live there half the year, I'll return back to the States to make a little money. And then I fly back to Fiji. Don't you want a family like that? The island guarantees their safety. It's a British colony after all."

"Sounds a little strange to me. I do admire your ambition, though. It's a great plan. I mean, it sounds like your plan is centuries old, but maybe you like that." "Yeah," said Cash, "but what about you? Don't you want to get married and have children?"

What he asked made my face harden and frown.

"I don't think I'll ever get married to a woman here," I said. "They're much too difficult. Going overseas is the answer, because no one wants to marry someone like me here in the States. There are too many complications. The women here are complicated. I'm too damn poor."

"So?"

"I'm going to try to make it alone. I'll be a good man, like I've always wanted to be, and I'll work hard for a while, retire when I move into a senior apartment complex, and I guess that's it."

"But what about your dreams?" asked Cash. "Don't you feel that you have to follow through? It's God's plan."

I could only grind my teeth, and say, "my dreams dried up a while ago. Life is suffering, and I see nothing remotely God-like about this country."

Cash put away his smart phone, and we returned to the task at hand. We returned from our secret fantasy worlds to the hardcore reality that prevented the many from following their dreams, as they get in line for one more day working like serfs for The Man on the Hill until the day was done.

Nevertheless, I was proud of Cash. He was a hard worker, and he kept his dreams instead of having to abandon them, like myself. He had the direction and the drive and the will to get to Fiji and carry out his plan. Even though his plans were a bit primitive, I realized then that the need to marry and procreate was a natural function governed by higher laws that didn't apply to me. I almost forgot how much of a loser I was, my past getting farther behind me - all of those fellow white people, the beautiful white women with skin like mine, going in many directions, never to connect again as we did at Trinity. Maybe that was a good thing? Who knew?

I felt comfortable working with Cash, and for a couple of weeks Cash and I picked up and hauled away as much junk as we could. We pleased the owner, but our wages were still pathetic. Cash and I laughed hard at the possibility that we would be hauling trash and living in the 'hood for the rest of our lives, and this, apparently, was God's plan for us, as it steered us far away from the worlds that we really wanted to belong to. We didn't want to be big shots at all. Fortune and fame seemed like the most shallow of all goals to achieve, but we still wanted a taste of it as well as the ability to escape from it and return to our miserable but honorable jobs of collecting junk off from the side streets, should we ever find ourselves in the least bit of danger from stardom. Cash and I were both obsessed with beautiful looking women.

"What are the women like in Fiji?" I asked.

"I think they are Black South Asians," he said.

"What makes you think they'll like you?"

"Any American is liked over there. Marry one, and you get to take her back to the States. But you? You're a white boy, and they go crazy over that. In fact, you're handsome and white enough that any country, other than this prudish one, would go ga-ga over you. You should know that before you get so down about yourself. No one is keeping us here except money. And once we get to Fiji, no one is going to get us to come back. If I'm a father, they'll even get pissed if I have leave for a little while. I also want to be a father too, y'know. An entirely tribe of people will have to rely on me."

"Sounds like you are trying to re-colonize the nation of Fiji."

"The key," said Cash, "is who does it first when America is on top."

"I don't get you, Cash. I just don't get you. You really want to fly to Fiji?"

"Damn straight!"

"I mean, don't you want to collect junk all your life? I can help you with that."

We both chuckled over this, and when the day was over, Cash and I decided to go to a bar where they had very pretty Irish college women running the place. Of course, we had to wake up early the next morning, as our jobs gave us very little time for leisure, but on this occasion, Cash and I affirmed that we were going nowhere, and there was no easy way to escape. Even while at the bar, Cash went on and on about Fiji, and while I hoped he got there, there was no way I was going with him.

He tried to convince me, but I knew better. I had to settle eventually in blue-collar Albany, where work seemed like the best bet.

I still wanted New England back though - those long summers in Provincetown, the fresh-water swimming holes, the Queen Bees with their sun-kissed, erotic bodies wearing skimpy bikinis. I liked all of that. And I thought that maybe if my father saw that I was working, then he'd lend me a little more just to have a future with his help. I must have thought of him a thousand times over. Even though I always needed more money, somehow I understood and respected his reasoning, as though I had turned as old as he had and grasped the same dubious principles of hard work, hard labor, and a simple life, just to avoid ruminating on what I deserved to have happen to me. Because if we saw the world arranged by merit, I would be at the top.

But it wasn't a world of merit. Far from it. It soon became a world of shortcuts and instant gratification. The people who receive all of these humanitarian awards were also the most flagrantly selfish, acting like assholes when the cameras couldn't locate them. It was a big trick to cover-up the unfairness, and if you stepped out of line, mighty forces would stick it to you in the back. Make no mistake about it.

I had to cut myself off from so much booze, though. I was working a beer-buzz when Cash ordered another round of drinks. The music was at a loud but conversational level, and he stared at the female waitresses who were hired for their looks. There was a lot of sausage at the bar, in other words. The interesting part of the night, though, was looking at these women, imagining being with them, and ordering more and more of their cocktails, which Cash insisted he pay for.

"At least let me have some dignity, Cash. I can pay for my share."

"You'll get me back later, when we both go to Fiji."

"Not this Fiji again, okay?"

"You're perfect for it, and since you are white, the women all over the islands will want you. I just know it."

"I don't want any children, Cash. Hell, I don't even want a girlfriend."

"Now that makes no sense at all. You're a handsome guy. You're not so poor, are you? Won't your parents leave you something?"

"I doubt it."

"But why don't you want a family, is what I'm asking?"

"I've seen the horrors and the suffering of the world. The struggle is too immense, wherever I go."

"Fiji is a breeze," said Cash. "We can have anything we want there."

"Sounds like you haven't read your Kipling yet."

"Who?"

"Just forget it. I don't want marriage, and I don't want children. That's just my way. That's the path I walk. It's too cruel out there, and for my son, it would be a nightmare. You take a young boy with a good heart, and the world mangles it up and twists it all around until it drains his blood. That's life, Cash. I see it. I see it now. All of these people working as slaves. I can't stand it. I'd rather sell heroin than have a child in this cauldron of a Hell. And that's how I see it."

We sat in silence at the bar for a while, sipping our drinks and watching the women walk by. They were like ghosts to me - a species that I saw from the past and how they betrayed me. They would never associate with a junk

65

dealer. They wanted the usual fare of doctors and lawyers, politicians, and Wall Street billionaires. They did not want me or my children, and maybe this was the price to pay for wisdom and experience in a world where people were just killing each other. Whether it was in the new Gulags of Russia, or even the propaganda that came out of the television that supported hawkish war stances, the only thing a man like me could do was to keep any child of mine far away from the damaged mess of civilization. And what was worse, most people already knew this and had children anyway, as though their own selfish needs had to be met first, some biological ticking bomb that had to rule over their bodies and over all that was reasonable and fair, until they had children - as though it were their duty to do so. How foul, I thought. How incredibly selfish. And now there was Cash with his unusual Fiji idea.

"Cash, I know that you mean well, but I think I have to bail on your Fiji plan. It doesn't seem like it's the move of a lifetime. Some people are just supposed to work and die. That's it. That's the trajectory of my life. Work and then die."

"God," he said, "you make it sound like a Nazi death camp."

"If you look through the cracks of this great nation, you can see the Nazi death camps returning."

"You know what I think?"

"What's that, Cash?"

"I think you're afraid, just like all of us. You want to be happy, but all you see is failure and people being tortured and dying. Who the hell put that into your head? I know that the junkyard didn't do it. We don't have it so bad."

"Where I come from," I said, "this place is pretty bad. I have peers that will be running the country, ruling the airwaves, bloated with so much money that it drives them mad. I have seen horrors that no one else seems to see. I consider myself damn lucky that we're able to have jobs, while most people must depend on these jobs just to feed their children."

"I don't know about you, Charlie. I really don't know about you. You're just so negative, and I can't figure out why."

"I'm always like this when I'm drunk, Cash. Believe me, it's nothing new."

Drunk and bleary-eyed, I wanted to drive Cash home. I didn't care if we were caught by the police or not. If we backtrack to thirty or forty years ago, the cops usually picked you up and brought you home if they caught you drunk on the roads. This was how society dealt with drunk drivers. And now?

People are forced into jails and pay thousands in fines.

This was why I had such a distaste for the older generation. They got away with everything in this country, and only after they pillaged and plundered the wealth of a nation do they write laws that prohibited every kind of unusual behavior that they themselves had committed. Shame on them, I thought.

Cash, however, was concerned. He said that I should sleep at his place until morning. But I wanted to drink more, and that meant being close to the fridge in my apartment. Nevertheless, Cash had to drive me to his apartment. I was way too drunk, and in the morning the work situation was horrible.

We're talking cold and flu and body aches, all capped off with the shame of nausea. It took Cash pouring a cup of cold water on me to get me out of bed and stumble to the shower - if only to dull the scent of the alcohol flowing out of my pores.

We went to the junkyard first. I vomited up most of what I drank the night before. Actually, I was still a little tipsy, and I also vomited a couple hours later. All I could do was pray that God made this a short day. Luckily, Cash told the boss-man that I was sick, and he let Cash drive me back home. At first, I needed help peeling my ass off of the passenger's seat, and once that was done, Cash walked me back to the apartment to see that I went to bed right away. I took some serious flu medicine to thwart the fever that so ruthlessly came up. I was in rough shape.

My apartment was an absolute mess with clothing all over the floor, the walls scratched and banged up with holes, the kitchen faucet unable to turn off despite how hard Cash had tried. He walked me to bed, and I threw myself on my tangled sheets that I hadn't changed in several weeks. The place smelled like a horse's stable.

"You need to clean this house," was the last thing that I heard Cash say before I passed out.

It was early afternoon. Cash pulled the blinds and turned on one of my oscillating fans. I must have slept for several hours straight, until I wet my bed and sweated out the remaining alcohol in my system. When my body responded this way, I started to feel much better. Unfortunately, I felt better at roughly two in the morning.

Nevertheless, I organized my clothes and money and did some tidying up. It didn't take very long. I did it quietly so I wouldn't disturb my neighbors. When the sun came up, I took another hot shower. Suddenly, a new day without sickness found me sputtering along, and when Cash visited with my truck the next morning, I was restored back to health. But Cash brought someone with him.

"Thanks for last night," I said. "I really owe you one."

"Don't think of it," said Cash. "You are a good egg, even when you're drunk. But I don't think you handle alcohol very well."

"I can hold my liquor," I said.

"No, I don't think you can. You drink fiercely, and then you don't stop until someone like me has to carry you home. Let's not drink anymore, okay? I like the better, sober version of yourself."

"And who's this," I asked of the woman who remained quiet in the back seat.

"Charlie, this is my old, good friend Gypsy. Gypsy, this is my good friend, Charlie."

We both exchanged greetings, as I reached my hand over my seat for a shake. She was a scrawny woman with hardly any breasts, but when our eyes met, I noticed they were blue. Her skin was beige, and her hair frizzed all about her. She looked small, almost like a child. I noticed how tangled her hair had become, and she didn't wear any make up. She had silver rings on the fingers of each hand, along with a gold necklace that spelled out her name. It dangled down her neckline. I had to stare a minute longer to determine her race. It turned out her father was black, and her mother was white. She looked like a fusion of the two and yet really very adorable all the same. I couldn't guess her age.

"What brings you to the junkyard, Gypsy," I asked, showing a very friendly and carefree side of myself.

I really didn't care what race she was. All of that college and prep school shit had ended. This was my real life. But before I could figure out anything else, Cash said,

"she's going to come to your house once a month to clean."

"What?"

"You heard me," said Cash. "Your house right now is disgusting. You're not taking care of yourself, Charlie, and I think you need a good, reliable maid to clean up at least once a month."

"I don't need a maid," I said.

"Really?" he asked. "When was the last time you mopped up the kitchen floor?"

"I don't recall."

"How about, how long ago did you vacuum your rug?"

"I don't recall that either."

"Well, Gypsy is yours for a low price every month."

"How much do you need, Gypsy?" I asked.

"Eighty-dollars a month," she said.

"How about sixty?"

"It's eighty or nothing."

"Cash," I said, "I don't think I can afford something like this."

"Will you take seventy?" asked Cash.

She thought about it for a few moments while biting her lower lip.

She wanted eighty, but she settled.

"Seventy it is," she said. "You just hired me as your new house cleaner. I'll do a great job for you."

"Sounds good, Gypsy," I said. "When can you start?"

"I can start tomorrow. First thing."

"There, you see!" said Cash. "Even the poor get to have maid service."

"Now I'm poorer," I said. "I don't plan to spend anything on leisure activities tonight. Most of my extra income will now go to

Gypsy."

"And your place will be transformed," said Cash. "By the time Gypsy is done, you'll feel proud of your place instead of it being something to get pissed off about. She works hard. She's good with cleaning. I think you'll really like her."

"Great."

Cash pulled up to a bus stop to let Gypsy off.

"Gypsy can handle it from here." And then to Gypsy, "but right now, Sweetie, I know you hate taking the bus. We're late for work."

"We're docked pretty heavily for lateness," I added.

"I get it," she said. "I'll take the bus home. I'll see you tomorrow morning, Charlie."

"Yeah," said Cash. "I'll pick you up tomorrow to take you to Charlie's. Okay?"

"Sounds good," as she hopped out of the truck.

We made it to work just five minutes shy of being handed our daily assignments. We were going to take a different route. We were to collect junk from people in Loudonville, which is a wealthy suburb of Albany. The trip was only twenty minutes, but I immediately knew that this small neighborhood had tons of money. The homes were stately plantation mansions and grand old colonials that stood within the middle of mowed acres of land. I honestly asked myself where in the world did these people get their money, and maybe I had made a big mistake by leaving school. If I were to get my degree now, it would cost me too much, as my family wouldn't have helped me out.

Once I left college against their advice, I was out on my own, and it didn't exactly feel like freedom either. Without money, I felt like a prisoner. I thought I could handle it, but I couldn't. I took one look at those stately homes and knew right away that I had lost whatever battle I had with my family. It seemed as though my parents were always right.

And whenever I decided on something important, I was always wrong. It just seemed that way.

After a warm day collecting junk in one of the wealthiest towns I had seen in the Capital District thus far, I became enraged by witnessing so many beautiful homes. I wasn't jealous necessarily. I was just angry. For me it was too late for learning. The more one departs from the academy, the harder it is to get back in there and get a degree. I could only throw my hands up in surrender on our drive back into Albany.

"What's wrong?" asked Cash. "You got so silent all of a sudden." "Just don't feel like talking," I said.

"C'mon, Charlie. That's not the Charlie I know. So spill it. Why are you upset all of a sudden?" "I've been upset all day," I said.

"Fill me in," said Cash.

"Well, I just can't believe what I've given up. One of those houses could have been mine if I hadn't left college."

"I see now. You miss your childhood riches. Is that right?"

"I've always been around money, even though I knew nothing about it. I don't know how to earn enough to get one of those houses in Loudonville. I can hardly afford the 'hood, and I'm just not used to it there either. I want what everyone else has."

"Maybe that's your problem," said Cash. "You want the stuff that you can't get anymore. You want to be rich again. Of course, I've never been rich myself, but I know it must be hard for a man who is rich to slide down the ladder of success and actually like where he lands. As far as I'm concerned, I'm comfortable these days. The 'hood is cheap too, which is nice. But Charlie, my man, you can't look back at the past. You have to look towards the future."

"I can't see any of it."

"You need to try. You don't want to be stuck in the past, do you? You have to know what you want to do to raise that kind of money, so you can afford a home like the ones we just saw. That's just the way it is. You have to have a plan of action, like me. I've got this idea about Fiji, and I know it will happen one of these days, just enough to buy that plane ticket there and back."

"I just…"

"Charlie, you and I are old enough to know that we can never go back. It wouldn't be the same no matter how hard we tried. To make that kind of money, you need to go to some school in the area. A vocational program. You should learn a trade, like car mechanics, or an electrician, or even a salesman at some big store. Selling cars, maybe. You can't expect to get to Loudonville on the backs of what the boss is paying us. You know that, right? We just haul away this junk. We get paid what the McDonald's people get. And God bless 'em. Their hard work is going to pay off, even though so many people make fun of them. But they know that they are really the leaders of tomorrow."

"Why don't we work at McDonald's then?"

"Hell, no. I'm sticking with this. At least we get to go outdoors and drive around."

When I drove my small truck back home that night, I fell asleep in my clothes. I was just plain exhausted. I was also a little depressed. I slid into bed, put the covers right over me, and fell asleep.

I slept so hard that I couldn't hear the doorbell ring the next morning. And then there was tapping at my window. I opened the blinds. It was Gypsy, the house cleaner, trying to get into the house. I hurried to the door and let her in. "Sorry about that," I said. "I was just sleeping." "No problem," she said.

I showed her to the cleaning products stashed below my kitchen sink. My apartment was so small, that it wouldn't take Gypsy much time to clean it. I'd say half-an-hour at the most. And suddenly, I felt like a sucker for giving her seventy bucks for the job.

When she walked in, the first thing she did was take off her sweatshirt and blouse. Her reed-thin body came out with a spandex tank-top that someone would wear to a gym.

There were breasts on her, but barely so. Her body was taut. In many respects, she was too skinny, and her hair was thick and messy. I didn't think much about her at the time. She wasn't a beauty to look at, that's for sure. But there was some attraction there. Not much, but some.

Gypsy dressed for warmth, but once in the apartment, she shed her clothes and was ready for work. It had grown warmer from the transition from a stultifying winter to a calm and even spring. Albany was lucky to have a spring, because usually the winter months are followed by a quick turnaround to summer.

I should have made myself scarce by taking a walk or going to the store, but when I asked if it was okay to lie on my bed and try to sleep as she cleaned, Gypsy had no problem with it. She went about her merry way, tank top and sweatpants, moving my shitty vacuum cleaner to and fro, up and down. But as I watched her, I suddenly found myself in a strange situation. Without much of her clothing on, I kind of wanted another kind of service. And when Gypsy caught me staring at her, she smiled and invited me to do something else, after she finished cleaning, of course.

I had gone without sex for some time now, and somehow, Gypsy brought sex appeal with her. I could tell that her bronze skin had been softened by the overuse of skin creme. Her legs were firm, her butt shapely, and she had a front that erased my memory of what I thought of her when we first met. All of a sudden, I was terribly attracted to this Gypsy just by watching her clean. When she rolled up the cord to the vacuum, though, I thought that the show had ended. But I was wrong.

"How'd I do?" she smiled.

I scanned the apartment for a moment and said, "you did fine."

"I usually do fine, yep. It's a great job, yep?" "It looks good," I smiled.

"Oh, you mean my body?"

"That too, yes."

"Y'know that cleaning isn't the only one service I provide for my customers."

"You clean many houses, then?"

"Not really. I have a side business."

She then did what I hoped she would do. The only place in the apartment to sit was on my bed. She hopped on it, and then grabbed hold of my loins.

"This costs extra," she whispered into my ear, her hot breath tickling my earlobe.

After we had sex, she got up from the bed, put on the clothes she had shed and said, "I guess I'll be seeing you next month. Take my number if you need anything. I'm available most of the time."

She gave me a business card that simply had her name on it, 'Gypsy', and her phone number.

"How are you getting home?" I asked.

"I have a ride coming. You should just take a nap, and I'll come over next time, okay?"

"Thanks for cleaning, Gypsy," I said.

"Aren't you forgetting something?" she asked.

It took me a few moments to realize that I hadn't paid her yet. I fished seventy more bucks out of my wallet and gave it to her. She counted it, smiled, and left the apartment. It was late afternoon now, and I should have rehired Gypsy for the other, secret services that she sold. I was left panting for her for some odd reason, because she wasn't exactly a person who would turn me on right away, but she did. I considered her an acquired taste that slowly crept up on me, like looking at gold and determining it real.

The nights grew tremendously lonely all of a sudden. Cash had things he had to do, his own plans, in other words. He had borrowed his uncle's car and got to work that way. While we still worked together on a few projects, we each were given our own separate assignments. Cash had been, after all, in training. It made sense that he could handle the loads on his own. I still thought about his Fiji idea, and how silly it was. But for Cash, it was very serious, and I tried not to poke fun or criticize it. A man had to follow his dreams, he said. At least he was doing something about it, while I, lacking the energy and the drive, could hardly pull myself out of bed every morning. Oddly enough, the only thing that was really going on in my life was Gypsy.

One night, after getting too sick of the television, I organized my wallet and found her card. I then called her. I didn't know what to expect. I left a message for her following a computerized voice greeting. I waited for a couple of hours. It was getting late, and I figured that she had other plans. I tried to get some sleep, and when I thought I was almost there, I heard the door buzzer ring. It must have been one in the morning.

I opened the door to find Gypsy, her blonde locks tumbling to her shoulders, her skin fully visible through a short, skimpy black dress that highlighted all of her curves. She was still skinny and still looked too young for her age, but by that time I didn't care much about what she looked like. I needed a woman in my bed and promised to pay her whatever she wanted. It turned out that there were costs for certain services.

The cheapest service was cuddling. I think that cost about forty bucks. The second was a hand-job. Sixty dollars. A blow-job came in third place with eighty dollars, followed by an all-inclusive package for a whopping one hundred and twenty dollars. She didn't come cheap, especially for the men she had hooked from her cleaning assignments. I gave her what I could. I reached down into my pocket and dragged out a crumpled seventy bucks. It was all I had until payday a couple of days down the road.

Once it was over, Gypsy got dressed and left. I kissed her mouth, because I appreciated it. She left in the early morning, after we both slept for a couple of hours.

In the early morning, I started up the truck and drove to the junkyard. Gypsy's late-night visit left me with only a couple of dollars to buy a cup of coffee. After that morning routine of stopping by a gas station convenience store, I was totally broke. I had no money, and that meant no credit cards or bank cards or checks. I was left with thirteen cents to ride out the day. I knew I was in trouble. I'd have to ask Cash for a loan, but he didn't seem like the type of person who loaned to friends.

Somewhere down the line we realize how useless it is for a friend to repay his debts. I was told on several occasions that if I lent money, good luck getting it back. A loan often meant giving the person the money instead of loaning it to him. Some may repay. Some may never repay. Regardless, it was better to keep one's own money than to loan it.

Even though I knew this full well, I still had to ask Cash for a twenty. I asked him when the work schedule finally permitted us to work together. We took the truck all around Albany, visiting the people who requested that we haul their junk away. We also remained scavengers ourselves by visiting the places in Albany where new junk was left on the curbsides.

"I need to ask you a favor, Cash," I said, after I found him checking out of the junkyard for the night.

"What do you need?" he asked.

"I need to borrow twenty bucks. Trust me, I'll pay you back, and I won't be asking you for money all the time."

Cash reached into his pocket where he stored a wad of cash. He peeled off a twenty and handed it to me."

"Thanks, man," I said. "I'm in a jam."

"Just don't do it too often, okay? I have bills to pay too."

"I understand."

The weekend came quickly, and I called Cash to see if he wanted to hang out. He couldn't due to a family event at a nearby church.

After a full Friday night alone, I knew that I needed to get out. Something about my life had to change, because somehow, many people all over the world seemed stuck between wanting to do something new and keeping a close eye on the affordability of doing something new, just like me. Most people in the 'hood couldn't afford anything. On a sunny, warmish Saturday, the black neighborhood folk sat outside on their front stoops that led up to their apartments and stoked up the fires for their weekly cookouts where their porch stairs met the pavement. I wanted to join them, and I probably could have, had I asked sincerely if I could join them. The truth was that I soon became jealous of them.

Even though we were all living in woebegone straits, the people that I saw seemed truly happy, as though all of those years of terrible history had been usurped by today's standards of comfortable living. In other words, they had evolved from the wreckage of a terrible past with high intelligence and a commitment to the many causes that floated around the Albany streets and affected their community. They could take a hard job and make the best of it, and I needed that type of intelligence and commitment. I needed their work ethic. I needed their happiness. All I could do that afternoon was watch them from my single window on the ground floor of my studio. I had deposited my paycheck in the bank that afternoon, and luckily, after I borrowed the twenty from Cash, the bank gave me credit for the check later that night. I knew that I needed Gypsy. I could use some cuddling for forty bucks.

I called her. She answered. She was on her way, as though sex were an emergency - and believe it or not, there are sexual emergencies that one experiences throughout one's life. After a few hours of waiting, I just needed to be close to a woman, I suppose, and that made me call her over and over again and also run into her voicemail every time. I would be spending almost half of my weekly paycheck on her. But I didn't care. I needed to wrap my arms around her, her tangled head at my chest. I could only pray for Gypsy to come over, and I had to wait for a couple of hours, simply pacing all over my small room, up and down, waiting for a phone call or the buzzer to ring, thinking about running my arm up her shirt, the comforts of her impeccably soft skin.

After waiting for about an hour, I guessed that she must have been busy. I was so tired from the long week of hauling junk, that I simply lay down on my bed and fell asleep. Gypsy showed up at two in the morning. Blurry eyed and weak, and also a little depressed, I answered the door.

Gypsy was there in a skin-tight dress, its length just covering up her wonderful buttocks - slim and taught. He hair was freshly combed. She looked like she just got out of a dance club and just decided to stop by my place, because she genuinely liked me. Of course, this wasn't true just yet, but she must have had feelings for me, considering that she showed up so late and could have easily blown me off.

"Hi," I said. "Welcome."

"I've got to freshen up," she said.

She headed straight for the bathroom. I heard the water running, first from the sink, and then from the shower. I expected her to take fifteen minutes at the most, but for some reason, she stayed in there for a very long time. When I knocked on the bathroom door, she said,

"I'll be a minute."

"Gypsy," I called through the door. "I'm about to fall asleep, and I have to use the bathroom."

"I'll be out in a minute," she called.

I had to wait for another half-hour before she emerged from the bathroom. I zipped in right after she had finished. When I came out, Gypsy sat on my bed, her legs open without any panties on and a smile on her face that was warm and inviting. I sat right next to her on the bed.

"I don't kiss on the first date," she said. "But you just want to cuddle, right?"

"Yeah. That would be nice right about now." "Forty bucks," she said.

I handed over what little I had, but after I gave Gypsy forty dollars, I was broke again and knew that there would be hell to pay the next morning. But I didn't care. We both lay on the bed, our clothes off, hugging each other like there was no tomorrow. And then I made the big mistake of leading her hand to my loins.

"That's another forty bucks," she said.

"What?"

"You heard me."

"The forty was the last I had."

"I know you're rich," she said. "Get some more money out of the ATM then."

"I don't have any money in the ATM."

"Then I guess we have a problem, then, don't we?"

"How am I supposed to get more money, and for what?"

"If I touch it, then it's an extra forty bucks."

"Now you tell me? Can't I pay you back at some point?"

"No. I need it tonight."

"Well, can't it wait until morning?"

"I'll sleep here then. I get the bed, and you get the floor."

I woke up stiff and uncomfortable from my night of sleeping on the torn carpet of my apartment. I had one blanket that covered me, and when I awoke after only a couple of hours, long after we finished our foreplay, she still slept soundly, her heavy breath moving in and out of her. That's the only fun I'd get for the rest of our time together. We only cuddled for five minutes, and then I made the big mistake of wanting more. I picked up the phone and called Cash.

"Good morning, *mon ami!*"

"*Mon* who?"

"It's Charlie. I'm at home."

"Kind of early for calling me on a Sunday morning, don't cha' think?"

"A little, yeah, but I have a problem."

"Now? It's only six o'clock in the morning."

"I know, Cash, but I have to borrow again. Gypsy spent the night last night, and she insists that I pay her more money, which is money that I don't have. Can I drive to your place and pick up a spare forty?"

"You're already a client of hers? Already?"

"Yeah."

"I thought it would at least take a couple of weeks, but you guys hit it off right away, eh?"

"Not exactly."

"How was she, by the way? For the twenty I loaned you, I hope you had a good time."

"It was strange. The whole thing felt strange. Plus, I hardly touched her, but she wanted forty more bucks just for touching me once. She's too expensive for me."

"I thought you guys would get along."

"It's not that. We do get along. It's just the money issue. She's got to bring it down a notch for me. Like you, I get paid once a week, which is not bad. But a good chunk of that goes to Gypsy. Can you talk to her for me?"

"You want me to ask her to lower the price?"

"Yeah. I still want to see her and all, but because she charges so much, I won't be able to stick with her. Can you do it?"

"I'll try. I'll call her tonight."

Over the next couple of weeks, I considered Cash to be my security. Rather than a bank account or a trust fund of any sort, Cash kept me grounded, and he started to lend me his good money, even though at times I didn't ask for it. I often wondered if Cash was the real millionaire in all of this.

I hung around with Cash as much as I could. With Gypsy, though,

I wanted to see her once a week, and without knowing how to pay Cash back, I borrowed from him once a week until I received my paycheck at the end of the week - most of which went to him. Because I wanted to see Gypsy, I was poorer than ever before. I bought a wholesale package of noodles for six bucks from the local warehouse store, and I tried to keep the apartment as warm as I could.

The landlords often skimped on the heat, so I had to buy a space heater. I went to a goodwill shop off of Central Avenue for a couple of pairs of pants and a few collared shirts.

I asked Gypsy to meet me again. She wanted forty dollars to pay from her ride from the nearby town of Menands. Cash told me that she lives there with her family. He also told me that she had a daughter. The custody of the child remained with her grandmother who must have found Gypsy's life too destructive to support a child. I was surprised, but it was true that Gypsy was let loose and kept away from the child, because of her lifestyle choices. I didn't have any problem with it, because I just wanted Gypsy. I didn't need the rest of her family, and what's more, she felt the same way. I could tell, though, that she made a lot of money while leaving me broke and scared of the risk that I may wind up in the local shelter.

She came early enough this time. I had just watched the seven o'clock news when I heard the buzzer. It was Gypsy at the front door. She looked a bit disheveled. Her hair was all over the place, and she wore layers to withstand the nighttime cold. She wanted forty dollars right away.

"For what?"

"I have to pay for my ride."

"That costs forty bucks? That doesn't make any sense. You're being cheated."

"Just give me the forty dollars. I'll be back in a second."

I gave her what I had, and she returned about five minutes later, harried from the outside winds. She brought a knapsack in with her and almost immediately, she headed straight for the bathroom. She must have been freshening up again. After a half hour of being in the bathroom, no matter how hard I tried to get her out by saying that I needed to go too, she wouldn't leave it.

"Just a minute!" she called.

I waited for an hour, and I held it in the whole time. I even thought of pissing in the sink, but I wasn't able to just yet. I still had some of my high-class education, and I thought to myself that no one would really piss in the sink, would they?

When she came out, she was ready for bed, ready for cuddling. I wasn't sure if I were ready to sleep with her again. I hardly even knew her. She looked really good to me, but I only had enough for cuddling. It was either that or spend the rest of my paycheck on her and ask Cash to lend me more come Monday. I gave her forty more dollars. She agreed that we should go farther than just cuddling.

With eighty dollars she relieved all of my stresses and pains of my experiences with the junkyard job. Sex really did relieve the accumulating stress, and I had never felt that relaxed before. This woman would do anything for money, which at first was good. But it all turned around when I had her sleep over.

After our fun and the depletion of my eighty dollars, she slept right next to me and spent the night. She fell asleep at around four in the morning. I watched her sleep, her chest rising and falling. I lay beside her, wrapped my arm around her naked body and easily fell asleep too, especially after waiting for so long. Unfortunately for me, though, I had to get up and work the next day.

It was a royal pain in the ass, I tell you. But I wouldn't be able to afford what little food I needed at the local store, had I not gone back to work. It seems like most people have hard work built into them. They carry it in their genes, and each new generation gets even more ferocious and competitive than the generation before it. I'm not a proponent of eugenics at all, but at the time, I started to look at people who had the genes predisposed for hard labor. They had been a part of the working world for generations, and suddenly, I may have been tossed out in the street, unable to do much of anything. It was a palpable fear that I had to live with almost every day. Perform or get cut.

Even the junkyard tired me. I wanted a raise, but at the same time, I didn't want to get fired. I noticed that the boss man began hiring a lot of other people for the same job I had, and soon their faces mixed in with ours. Most of them were immigrants, so the boss-man saved on labor costs. If I asked for a raise, I would be cast out of the junk hauling business, which would mean the downtown Mission would be my next home.

Yes, poverty here sucked that much, even though I am much older now. There's no living wage, just hard laborious work that white-collared people in the suburbs subsidized with their property tax dollars. I'm not really sure how it happens. I'm much more accepting of it these days, but whenever I had a shitty job, like hauling away junk, I had become used to long hours and the minimum wage earnings I painfully saved for a rainy day. Basically, I lived paycheck to paycheck.

At the end of the month, I made sure that I didn't spend beyond my humble means. And I also missed my friends from Exeter. I even missed Trinity, even though I was there for a very short time. I had to get over the idea that some God would rescue me and return me to these elite places, but this just wasn't going to happen. The people that I knew and the hockey friend that I had met while in New England were indelible memories stamped onto my mind, and the longer I worked, the more I missed these old places and faces.

The junkyard soon seemed like a United Nations meeting. This is how the boss used diversity to make the company. He would save plenty of money. Too many white people were just too expensive. Instead, we soon had people who would break their backs for minimum wage, while I simply skated along waiting for Gypsy to call me, after I called her.

"I'll be right over," she said on the phone.

Cash refused to lend me more for Gypsy. Not only was Cash tapped out, he said that I should pay him back in full before he lent me another penny. I was still thankful for him, though. He had loaned me plenty of money over the past few months, and I gathered together just enough money for cuddling that night.

She knocked on the door after I patiently waited for her. She again came in around midnight, just a few minutes before I had drowsily dipped into sleep, but I awoke on full tilt, waiting for some stress relief. That's what we called our encounters - 'stress relief.' And, boy, was I stressed out.

I let her in, and she went straight to the bathroom. I heard the water running. I tolerated the first few minutes of the use of my bathroom. Once again, though, she took an hour, and I was getting sleepy as hell. I figured out that we were on different time zones. She woke up at night, stayed awake, and then went to bed in the early morning. I was the opposite. I'd wake up early and then go to work. I'd shower at night.

I'd knock on the bathroom door plenty of times, and at times she'd respond, "just a minute!". At other times during the long wait, she wouldn't respond at all. I banged on the door harder and harder as her bathroom use persisted. I had work in the morning, and I was tired of waiting for her.

Finally, I just barged into the bathroom to find her doing some kind of yoga-type stretching in front of the bathroom mirror. She didn't even recognize I was there.

Her concentration on the movements were such that she blocked everything out, which included my voice. I told her I wanted her out of the bathroom, but she quietly stretched her body, as though in some trance or in submission to the universal power of womanhood. I couldn't understand it. I simply closed the door and let her do all of the mystical rituals she wanted. She must have picked them up from another culture, I wasn't sure. I decided to leave her in there, as I slipped into bed without any clothes on and prayed she would get out of the bathroom.

It must have been ten in the morning when she woke me up. I was late, and I declared the day done. I wasn't sure if the boss-man would fire me or not for it. She wanted money for the cuddling session, so I paid her yet another forty bucks. She climbed in, and without doing anything else, she cuddled for a while. I was really hoping for more, because I had another twenty-dollar bill hanging around somewhere in my dresser. She, however, fell asleep while cuddling. I did too. She slept in my bed the whole day, and left for a night just before I fell asleep.

The next morning, I had no other choice but to leave Gypsy in my bed again while I went to work. I was nervous about leaving her there, because I didn't know her well enough then. Nevertheless, I did leave her in my bed and begrudgingly went on my way.

I returned after seven hours of driving around all parts of the Capital District and hauling away heavy metal for the boss-man. When my day was finally over, I returned to the apartment, only to find my television gone. There were also a few clothes that were missing. Gypsy must have stolen them. Yet before jumping to any conclusions, I called Gypsy. But no answer. I couldn't believe she took my television. And then I asked myself, why would I ever have listened to Cash for social advice. Don't get me wrong. The man who l gets to lie next to a woman at night is blessed and lucky indeed, but my television? My clothing? I was pissed off. I tried Gypsy again.

"Hello?"

"Gypsy, this is Charlie. I have a bone to pick with you. Did you take my television and some of my clothes?"

"I had to," she said in her raspy voice. "You didn't have enough money."

"What are you talking about? I gave you all I had."

"Yeah, but you forgot the overnight fee."

"What overnight fee?"

"The fee I charge for overnight visits."

"Are you mad?! You never told me about a fee for overnight visits."

"Well, now you know," she said.

"I want my television back. I want my clothes back to."

"You have to pay me to get them back."

"What? Do you think I'm rich or something? Money doesn't grow on trees. I'm living like a pauper here. I have no money. That's why I have to take a shitty job at a junkyard."

"It's too late anyway. The television is gone."

"Fine. Don't call here ever again, or I'm calling the police."

"Okay."

She hung up the phone, and I punched another hole in the wall of my studio. I loved that television. It was the only real activity I had been left with - a chatter box that kept me company, advertising propaganda that kept me striving for more and more and more, and the images on the screen, many of which I could just sit in front of and space out to.

Suddenly, there was even more loneliness where loneliness had already been. Add to that my desires for the woman. I called Gypsy again after work, because I wanted her in my bed.

"Okay, Gypsy," I said on phone. "You win. Can you come over tonight?"

"I need forty for my driver."

"I think I'll just starve."

"What was that?"

"Nothing. It's not important. But can you come over? I'm feeling a little under the weather, so I need you to restore me back to health."

"I'll be over soon, sweetie," she said, before hanging up the phone.

And, again, I waited for her to arrive. I waited for her a couple of hours at least. She knocked on my door at one in the morning. I doubted that I'd be able to work at the junkyard if Gypsy kept showing up so late.

She basically barged in. She carried a small bag filled with her own clothes. And, as usual, she headed straight for the bathroom. I tried to stop her, but she was much too quick for me. She went in, locked the door, and did what? I wasn't sure. It was probably the same yoga positions in front of the bathroom mirror again. She even took a shower in between.

She emerged from the steamy bathroom looking all dolled-up. I decided then that I needed to sleep with her, and yes, this would cost a lot of money, but what could I do? I hungered for her. I pained for her. I had a hard-on for at least an hour, and I was ready to roll. I gave her all the money I had, even the stuff that I had tucked away for the last several months in a secret hiding place. She looked good - legs taut, although very little breast action, and some of the smoothest skin I've ever felt.

I slept comfortably that night with our bodies entwined. I didn't jolt awake at three in morning on a random search for food. Instead, Gypsy woke me up at four ayem. At first, I thought it was a dream, but the more Gypsy poked and prodded me, the more cognizant I became that she wanted something.

"Gypsy, what are you doing?" I yawned.

"I need some money."

"What?"

"I need some money."

"I don't have any money."

"Yeah, you do."

"I'm saying, I don't have any."

"Don't lie. I know you have some."

"No."

"Yes."

"No."

"Yes."

We went on like this for a while, until I had to look in my secret hiding place for whatever savings I had put away. I told her to leave the room. I found forty dollars underneath my mattress. I offered it to her, after I called for her return.

"How am I supposed to survive, then?" I asked.

"You won't have a problem with that."

"Gypsy, I'm not a millionaire."

"Yes, you are."

"What makes you think so?"

"Charlie, stop insulting my intelligence."

"I'm not insulting anything. Why do you think I'm a millionaire?"

"I just know, okay."

"Look at this place. I live in the 'hood. People on these streets get killed every day. It's the most dangerous place in Albany. Look at my apartment. It's a shoe box."

"Charlie, stop insulting my intelligence!"

"I'm not insulting your intelligence. How do you know I'm so rich then, if I am indeed rich?"

"I just know."

"That's not good enough. What is making you think that I'm a millionaire?"

"It's your look. That white look. I can tell right away.

Your family is rich."

"My family practically dropped me off here. They shooed me away. Their own money is their own money. They don't give me a dime of it."

"I can tell."

"Fine. Here's the rest of it."

I gave her whatever I had, which was a scant little to what I had started the week with. She put it away in her secret hiding place, which was in her purse, and then slipped back under the covers with me. We cuddled for a while, until she let me go all the way. Her thin frame was on top of me, and we just made love until the dawn's first rays, which came about an hour later.

When I slipped out from her body that had fallen over me, I found remarkable how the sheer ecstasy of having her in my bed warmed my whole body, but then directly afterwards, the cold reality sunk in that I had no money left, and that I would have to go hungry for a few days until I received my next paycheck. I wasn't going to ask Cash for more money. Instead, I would try being as frugal as possible, which wasn't exactly my forte.

Gypsy was only half-right. My parents did have money. I, however, did not. I explained it to her a number of times before she left in the early morning and went back to wherever she came from. I had to ask for an advance on my paycheck. I couldn't starve myself for a few days. I needed that advance.

After I finished work that day, I went up to the busman's office and had a word with him.

"What's up, Charlie?" asked the boss-man. "You look beat."

"I am, sir, I really am."

"The day is over. Go get some sleep. Have a good weekend."

"I have to ask you something."

"What is it then? I hope it's not a long conversation."

"I need an advance on my paycheck."

"An advance? We don't give out advances. You'll have to wait for payday."

"I need some money. Please, can I at least borrow some money?"

"It's a policy. That's how it works. Now come back to work on Monday. There's a lot of junk out there. I can tell that you haven't been collecting much lately."

"I'm working on it," I said, "and thanks anyway."

"You'll get your paycheck soon enough."

There's nothing quite like starving. Cash had invited me out for drinks, but I had to decline. I couldn't bring myself to ask him for money again. I had a couple dollars in quarters, and that's about all I had. I spent it on fast food.

Good, cheap, and terrible for the entire body. Nevertheless, I had to make the best of it. I could hardly get to sleep that night, because there was no soda or beer in my fridge. I to rely on lukewarm tap water.

Watching television had always perturbed me anyway. All they had were local commercials for steak houses and restaurants, and oh, I could have used a good steak right then and there, melting in my mouth like butter, that end-of-all taste of precious meat that at one time fed armies and legions. I called the only one able to furnish me with more funds, and that was Gypsy.

"Can I hit you up with a loan, please. I'm starving around here. I couldn't even get to sleep last night. That, or you could at least buy me breakfast at the diner on Central Avenue."

"No," she said. "I don't have any money."

"But I just gave it to you last night. What could you have possibly done with it?"

"It's gone."

"Well, that's just great. But listen, Gypsy, I need just a few dollars to get something to eat. I'll never ask you again."

"Sorry, Charlie. I don't have any."

"Gypsy! I gave you a bunch of money last night!"

"Call me when you get your paycheck."

She hung up the phone after that. I just couldn't believe, after all I had given her, that she wouldn't lend me at least a few dollars. I felt like dying, the lukewarm tap water making me sick to my stomach. Oh, how I hated ordinary water way back then. Then, I suspected something about her, but this definitely wouldn't generate any money for me.

I still wondered, though, how on God's green Earth she could have spent all of that money in just a few hours.

I walked into my bathroom where Gypsy had her yoga trances, and I looked all around the place. I checked the medicine cabinet, the storage space under the sink, and even the garbage bin. It was only until I checked under the radiator that I found two used crack pipes.

I finally learned where all of her money went. Aside from being a mediocre house cleaner, Gypsy was also a drug addict. Most of her money must have gone to that cause. A wave of anger shot through me just then, but then I thought that since Cash was the one who introduced me to Gypsy, he may feel poorly about it and lend me a few bucks.

I tried that line of argument that afternoon, and sure enough, Cash loaned me another twenty. He said that he couldn't support me, as a father might support a child. At the same time, though, he did feel badly that he introduced me to Gypsy. He must have known about her side business, but

103

perhaps he was giving her a chance to hold a job for once. I often forgot how Cash generally helped people out. By introducing me to Gypsy, he must have known that I needed the help, and she must have needed the work. It was a win-win situation for him as far as his spiritual drive to help as many people as he could. Cash immediately took me to fast food. He bought me a breakfast sandwich, which definitely helped my insides, even though it had very little nutritional value. I didn't care. My belly needed filling.

"I'm sorry about all of this, Charlie."

"You don't have to be sorry. She's a really tough person when it comes to money. She wouldn't even lend me any to get through the weekend. What am I supposed to do now?"

"I can take Gypsy away, if you'd like. There are plenty of people in this town who need house cleaners. Seriously. There's a shortage."

I had to make a decision there: to have Cash take away Gypsy, or I could stick with Gypsy but not see her so regularly.

"What's done is done, Cash. I still want Gypsy to clean the apartment."

"I know why you want to keep her," he smiled. "But if you can't afford her, you can't afford her."

"I don't want her to leave, Cash."

"Wait one minute. Even though she took all of your money and stole your television set and some of the high-priced clothes in your closet, you still want to see her? I don't think it's a smart move, unless, unless, of course, you have feelings for this woman."

"I can only afford her once a month. That's all I can do."

"I'll let her know," said Cash. "That way, you won't spend all of your money on her. You actually like this woman? Really?"

"Yeah, sure," said Charlie. "She could use some help with her cleaning methods, though."

"You mean by having two women come over?"

"No. I don't mean it that way. She should enhance her cleaning skills while with me, that's all."

"Charlie, I hate to tell you this, but those side businesses that Gypsy has? She is mostly known as a prostitute. That's actually where she gets her money, and then she blows it all on crack."

"I found her collection of crack pipes in the bathroom."

"I never thought she'd act up again like that. The whole intention was to get you a girl to clean that pig sty of yours, not a good cleaning woman to sleep with you every time you needed her"

"So that's why you did it?"

"Yeah. I thought she'd stay just clean for just one day and vanish. But what you have to do now is get rid of her. I put the ball in your court, because I never expected this would happen. I know it's my fault, so I guess I can lend you some money, only time to time, until you fire her from the cleaning position. Think about it. It's in my own interests to have you cut her off. I can't lend you money forever, man."

"I'll take care of it, Cash."

"As soon as possible, if you can. Here. Here's another twenty.

Don't ask me again until a full week has gone by."

With Cash lending me money, I could now afford to get by, albeit meagerly. She took all of my money, my television, my clothes, and the oddest part about this arrangement was that I still wanted to see her. She wasn't a very good house cleaner, but in bed she was the best. I needed her, and I asked myself why.

After Cash alerted me, it became full-on obvious to me that Gypsy was indeed a sex worker. I like the term *sex worker* instead of the older terms, like *whore, hooker, prostitute* and what usually followed this antiquated and faulty type of rhetoric. I committed myself to respecting all women at all times, and Gypsy was one of those women.

Yet, when I called her over, she always wanted all the money I had.

She came convinced that I was a millionaire, even though I insisted that I was not. Sometimes we'd wrestle in bed, because I wouldn't give her the money that was due, at least not right away anyway. I put the money in the underwear I wore around the apartment.

"Stop playin' with me, Charlie!" she would yell.

And when she came over this time, there was nothing to do but have sex and listen to the radio. I couldn't do anything but follow her around within my box-like apartment. And I mean, literally following her around the kitchen area where she made rice and beans. She would yell at me on that crime as well. No longer could I follow her. She accused me of being a child.

Somehow, I learned to like arguing with her. We argued mostly about money. What else do couples really argue about anyway? But to get the point, with help from Cash, I was able to see Gypsy once a week. This satisfied me. Regardless of her time spent in the bathroom or wrestling her on the bed until she found my money, I had to admit at the time that we felt like we were both playing around. I had fun wrestling with her and making her life annoying. If anything, I was annoying to her after a little while. But we still wrestled until she found the money I had tucked away. She would yell at me and punch me in the arm. Somehow, I was slowly falling for this woman.

"I know your body," she said after a month of seeing her.

She was right. She learned what I needed sexually, and she did exactly what I needed her to do in bed. For some reason, I really didn't care if she stole from me. There was the obvious attraction I had towards this nightmare waif, but I did begin to care for her. It was as though she relied heavily on the money that I gave her each week. After we were done making love one night, she admitted that she had twenty misdemeanors.

"How on Earth can one woman get twenty misdemeanors?"

"I'm serious. I have twenty of them."

"What did you do?"

"Mostly shoplifting. They put me in jail a little while, but once I was done, I stopped doing what I was doing."

"So, you are an unsuccessful thief? Why am I not surprised by that?"

"Shut up, Charlie."

"I ought to turn you in for using drugs and stealing from me."

"That won't do it."

"Oh, yeah? Why not?"

"Because I know most of the cops in this city."

"You? Ha!"

"I provide my services to them."

"You're kidding, right?"

"No. I've serviced cops before. They all know me. They don't arrest me anymore. I'm good for the department, stupid."

"Have you ever thought about quitting all of that? Maybe finding a real relationship? Moving away and starting all over again?"

"You mean, the American Dream?"

"Something like that."

"Well, I'm going to school for welding. Classes start pretty soon."

"Welding? You? You're too frail for being a welder. The equipment is probably much heavier than you are."

"Shut up, Charlie."

We would pillow talk this way, until it came time to surrender whatever dollars I had. We slept soundly that night, and because I had developed feelings for her, especially the feeling to protect her lightweight and small frame of a body from the cold nights of Albany, I asked her back almost every couple of nights, just to make sure she was

109

safe while street-walking. It was funny, because when she was doing business out on the street, the johns would pay her much less for it than I had to pay. I often wondered if she was collecting more money from me than justified. This struck me as odd, because I thought she had feelings for me as well.

One night, she refused to leave the bathroom. I had to go pretty badly, and no matter how much I had pounded on the door, she wouldn't leave. I tried pushing the door open, but she would immediately push back, as though the bathroom was suddenly hers. I followed through on the threat to call the police. I said this to Gypsy a number of times, but I was being ignored.

Within ten minutes, the cops had arrived, but not before Gypsy vacated the bathroom just before I let them in the front door. The cops were little pissed, since there was nothing wrong anymore. But they questioned Gypsy, and they knew that she was whacked out on crack. It didn't matter, though. Gypsy had formed a city-wide network of safe people and places where she could go, to avoid jail especially. The cops wouldn't say it, but it was obvious to me that they knew Gypsy, or at least knew of her, as she seemed to be a household name for cops while out on the beat at night.

There was also the time she claimed that I stole twenty dollars from her. And this was a twenty-dollar bill that I had given to her right when she walked in. I had to call the cops again, because she wouldn't leave the apartment before I had to go to work. I didn't trust here to stay all alone by herself. By this time, she had been storing her things in my apartment. Surreptitiously, she caused this kind of trouble, and I remember calling the cops a number of times, just to get her out of the apartment, since I couldn't trust her to be there. She might have taken everything, if I left here in there for too long. The cops answer to this?

"Just pay her the twenty dollars that she claimed she lost. Would that be acceptable to you?"

Hell, no! But I surrendered another twenty-dollar bill to replace the one she lost. I was the one who lost, and once the police left, I neared a doom of sorts. Gypsy played me for a weak sucker.

"If you want to come over, you have to stop stealing from me. I don't know why I'm letting you in now."

"I don't steal, stupid."

I talked to her while following her into the apartment kitchen.

"Stop aggravating me, Charlie!"

"Gypsy, I need some stress relief."

"No! Give me forty bucks first." "Alright," and I surrendered forty dollars.

"Okay, now is the time!" I said excitedly.

Where did Gypsy go next? Straight to the bathroom.

I'm no fool. I knew she smoked crack in there, but these yoga stretches had to go. They took a lot of time. And so, I banged and banged harder on the door. After about a half-hour, she emerged. She had apparently washed her hair in the sink and smoked enough crack to satisfy her impulses to mask any pain she must have been carrying around with her.

I ran into the bathroom, did my business, and when I came out, Gypsy was sitting on my bed, making phone calls. She texted a lot.

She went on texting for another half-hour. I bothered her here and there so that she wouldn't pay attention to her smart phone, but only to me. She wasn't having it. I waited for over an hour for her to touch me, but she didn't. She took my forty dollars and simply ran away. After I got home from work the next day, she called me.

"Hi, Charlie!" she said. *"What ya doin'."*

"Nothing with you."

"Can I stop by?"

"No."

"Please? I know your nuts are stressed out. I can relieve them for you."

"I'm not interested in sex with you anymore, okay? I'm broke."

"Oh, sure you are. That's what you always say."

"I'm serious. I have no money. You can come over here if you want to, but there is no money here. What time are you coming?"

"About a half-hour."

"Liar! You'll probably take three hours. I have to wake up for work in the morning."

"A half-hour is all I'm asking," she said.

"Fine."

And I hung up the phone. This time she came at two in the morning. It took roughly four hours for her to make it to my apartment, when she lives much closer than that. I surmised through my tattered mind that Gypsy must have been buying crack with it.

Normally, most men would end the relationship right away, but there was something about her. I needed her as a friend, and I'm still not sure why I needed her. It became obvious to me that she deserved some kind of care and protection to deal with the cold temperatures, tests for venereal disease, the simple need to eat at least one meal per day. She wasn't eating properly. She had lost even more weight to keep her body skinny when it was easy to see that she needed to gain weight, not lose it.

She shot straight to the bathroom, as though my apartment were a rest stop along a highway. She stayed in there an hour. Knocking on the door and yelling for her to get out became this twisted routine of ours. She won all the games we played, whether that were wrestling or hitting me up for money, or even insisting that she get more Diet Cola from the bodega down the street. When she emerged and went into my bedroom, I was glad that I caught her there.

"Charlie, I need forty dollars."

"Excuse me?" "I

need forty dollars."

"Don't have any," I said.

"Don't lie."

"I'm not lying. I don't have forty dollars."

It was four in the morning, and I hadn't gotten a wink of sleep. Instead, I'm arguing with Gypsy about whether or not to give her the remainder of the money I had, just for her to go away. I didn't want to see her anymore, even though she looked so waifish in the light of my bedroom, that I thought she had suffered through a famine. I had to break up with her. I didn't get away with saving my last forty dollars, though. I was so tired arguing with her, that I simply surrendered my only twenty.

"Gypsy, now I need some money. I'm nearly three days away from payday."

"I don't have it," she said.

"But I just gave you twenty yesterday. I need some of it back to buy noodles and soda."

She left after that, after she tucked the money into her bra. She clarified that the twenty I gave her was probably the only thing she cared about while dealing with me.

"This is the last time I'm going to see you, Gypsy. I don't want any more of your money-hungry ways. I give you all this money, and you can't spare any for me to get something to eat?"

"Shut up, Charlie. I'm the only one around here who knows your body. No other woman does. You'd have to start all over again."

I considered this a huge point scored in her arsenal of sex worker wisdom. She was right. We had been having sex for so long now, that I often wondered if I were still capable of loving someone else. Thus far, I haven't had to look at any other women. I didn't need to be that only scumbag at the bar pinching women's asses. I had no need to get drunk or painfully talk to beautiful female strangers on the streets of Albany. And yet, I didn't want to remain with Gypsy any longer. For these reasons, I had to rely on Cash.

"What the hell do you from with me?" asked Cash, when I saw him before we all left for junk collection out in the city of Albany.

"This won't happen again."

"Listen, man. I can no longer support you. I don't have any money myself. I'm starving too."

"How about we go get a meal. At McDonald's or Burger King? I'm just thinking that you're hungry, and you'll feel better about things if you ate first."

We both had our own trucks now, and we both agreed that we could afford to eat. We met at the nearest McDonald's on South Pearl Street. It was open twenty-four/seven. He paid for my breakfast, but I still needed some more dough for the essentials of diet soda and cigarettes.

When we sat down, I canvassed the several workers behind the counter. They were busy, and they worked hard. And here I was, an Exeter man, asking Cash for more money, while looking behind the counter and seeing these whole black faces working hard. I couldn't even do what they were doing. I realized just then that fast-food jobs were an incubator for successful people. They had the work ethic down, and in the job market, once finished with the fast-food industry, these young people would be ready to think hard at college and work hard on the job. I was impressed. But Cash had to bring me down a little. He saw that I was spacing out.

"Earth to Charlie," he said. "Earth to Charlie. Come in Charlie."

"Sorry, Cash. Anyway, as we were talking about, I need some money to tie me over until Saturday."

"It's Gypsy again."

"Yes," I said. "She bullies me into paying her. I have to give her money just so she goes away."

"But then you keep calling her?"

"She calls me, and entices me to let her over. When she calls, I must admit, I get too horny. I let her in because I want her company. She uses my bathroom to make herself pretty and does some crack. She asks for money, and she doesn't return right away. She takes a couple of hours. And meanwhile, I'm sleeping soundly, until waken up by my terrible buzzer from downstairs, and there she is again. It's maddening."

"You can get a restraining order?" asked Cash. "And as we know already, I was the fool who put you two together. I had no idea you'd go this far with her."

"I thought about getting a restraining order too, but I don't want her to go to jail. I have feelings for this woman too, y'know."

"Oh, shit, Charlie. Are you telling me you're in love with her? Or anything close to that?"

"I'm not in love with her. I just feel that it's too cold to be standing out on the sidewalks in the dead of night. It's too dangerous for her to be smoking all that crack. She's a druggie for Christ's sake, and one of these days she's going to find herself shut out of everything except a cold metal jail cell."

"Have you thought that maybe that's the best way to save her life? Y'know, prison is terrible. I agree, but she needs tough love to find her way out of the lifestyle she leads. If you have to shut her out, Charlie, you better shut her out, even if you do have feelings for her. It sounds like you're too soft. You have to assert yourself."

"I know, but I like her."

"Well, that's all the advice I'm going to give you. Here's forty. That should get you through until Friday. Just don't forget to pay me back. As far as Gypsy is concerned, get a restraining order and have her arrested if she violates it."

"Thanks for the money, Cash."

"The only way I'll accept your thanks is if you get rid of her."

"Understood."

That night, I definitely didn't want to call Gypsy. More of her clothes had been stored at my place. There were also toiletries that went missing. It was always the little things - the last bar of soap, a charger for my phone, a nice pair of gloves, the last of my toilet paper. She took the little things, and I just about had had enough of it. I was glad she didn't call that night, and I hoped that she'd extend the time we had been apart. But she would always show up after I had gotten paid every Friday. She knew to call that night, regardless if I were broke already. She picked up my routines quickly and struck just

when I thought I could pay Cash everything back on Friday. I owed him a lot, and I didn't want ruin my friendship with him.

"Hi, Charlie. Did you miss me?"

"Not really, no. You really have me in a tough bind."

"Are you stressed out?"

"No. I no longer have the need to see you. I'm sorry, Gypsy, but don't come over here ever again. I don't want to lose you as a friend, though. But it would be better for everyone involved if you didn't come over here anymore."

"I know you need stress relief."

Add to this that I missed her. Just arguing with her would do, the wrestling on the bed when I wouldn't give her any money at four in the morning, the apartment that I paid for her to clean, which resulted in nothing more than even more of a mess. And yet, I wanted to see her, because maybe times had changed. Maybe I didn't need to give her any more money.

"I need forty dollars for the ride."

"Yeah," I said, "and then you take everything I have. And even if you steal things from me, you are unable to lend me money when I need it. That is not a friendship. That's just plain old sex work. You're not fooling anyone. And what kind of ride do you need just get over the Hudson. A cab would cost twenty. What you really want, though, is that crack you smoke."

"And what about you? You have a job in a junkyard. You're not even in my league. I deal with rich and important men."

"Then why don't you believe that I don't have anything to give you? I'm not a rich or important man. Actually, the direct opposite is true. Can't you understand that? Money doesn't fall from trees.

How far are you away?"

"I'm about ten minutes away. I can give you total stress relief for forty dollars."

"Ok, then. Come on over. Might as well, since you're only ten minutes away."

I waited an hour. She still didn't arrive. I was in a rage. I wanted to call her and tell her that I didn't want to see her anymore. It wasn't worth the aggravation and the theft and the occupation of my bathroom. I wanted a normal relationship. I wanted to marry a woman like the I once had at Trinity. I strongly thought that I should just tell my parents that I wanted to go back to college. Sure, I was older, and maybe my intellect wasn't as sharp as it used to be. Nevertheless, I had to call the college and see if they would take me back. For now, though, I waited for Gypsy.

It was getting later and later into the night. I paced, I called her cell phone a number of times, I even slept a little. She finally arrived at three in the morning. I had to be at work in a couple of hours.

When I did hear a knock at the door, I went up close to it and said, "go away." I wanted her to leave a long time ago. No more would I put up with Gypsy.

"Charlie, open the door."

"Go home, Gypsy. This is the last time I want to see you here."

"Stop playing with me, Charlie. Let me in."

"No."

"Yes." "No.

"Yes."

And this binary exchange of yeses and noes only got louder. As the volume of our voices escalated, I had to be mindful of my neighbors at three in the morning. Gypsy kept on talking loudly on the other side of the door. I didn't want any noise complaints. With a deep sigh, I let her in. Where did she go? Straight to my fucking bathroom.

I had grown used to it. It didn't make me upset anymore. I fell asleep for about an hour. I didn't care if she relieved my stress or not, because Gypsy had become the source of that stress. By the time she had crawled into my bed, I had to get up to shower for work. She fell asleep easily, but now I faced another dilemma. I couldn't leave her in my apartment all day. She might have stolen everything out from under me. I didn't want to call in sick either. I had to wake her up and ask her to leave. I didn't exactly look forward to this.

First, I turned on the overhead light. Second, I hovered over her thin body which slept soundly on my bed. She had the habit of covering up her body in its entirety - even the face and the head. So, thirdly, I ripped the covers off and shook her awake, and like a spring, her arm snapped back on me and hit me in the thigh.

"Gypsy, you really do have to go. You can't stay here while I'm at work."

"Don't worry. I won't steal anything."

"I would like to believe that, but now that you have stolen my flat screen television, a couple of tablet computers, and the many small things that mysteriously go missing, having you here is not a good idea."

"Just shut up, Charlie."

"Hey, I can't leave unless you leave. I'm already getting late for work."

I missed work that morning. I called in sick, and it was all Gypsy's fault. She would not get out of my bed.

In a half-sleep, she said, "I need to get some clothes at the store."

"That's great news, Gypsy. Maybe you could get out of bed and do it."

She still didn't want to get out bed, so I put some cold water from the fridge in a pot and poured it all over her.

"What the hell were you doing, Charlie!"

"I called in sick because of you"

"So, this is how you wake me up?! What the hell is the matter with you?!"

"You can't stay here. You have to leave. No one will be around to watch you."

"You just called in sick, though? We should go to the store, you asshole. I need some new clothes."

"No, Gypsy, you have to go to the store to pay for your own damned clothing. I, however, have no reason at all to go shopping with you. Generally, I'm not that into clothes, but if you go on your own, that would be best."

Still no dice. She wanted me to take her there. It was as though I had to pay her to leave the apartment, just to get her off my back. It was a wasted day anyway as far as work was concerned. I thought that she'd buy a couple of items at the department store, but once again, I had to pay for these clothes, and when I did, she showed her affection by biting my ear at the checkout counter. She reserved this affectionate ear-biting for those who bought things for her. Somehow, I was now included on this insane list of damaged men who probably already had Gypsy's small bite marks on their ear. What a club we would make, with Gypsy reigning over us as our Queen.

I was lucky to get out of the mall that morning. It was high noon by the time we paid the floater-cashiers who miraculously showed up at an unoccupied cash register. Eventually, we did get a cashier, and then I was very lucky to get out of the store that led into the mall. Before we could leave, though, a security guard stopped us and asked Gypsy to come to his office.

"But why?" I asked. "Did she do something wrong?"

"Mind your own business, you," said the guard.

"Wait here, Charlie," she said. "I'll be back soon."

I looked around the department store. The prices were too high, and I couldn't even purchase a pack of new underwear. I wanted to get out of the store as soon as I could, but then I waited for a full hour until the guard released Gypsy. I saw her with a shopping bag. The guard did not follow her to the mouth of the department store. Only Gypsy emerged.

"What the hell happened? I've been waiting a whole hour. And what's in your shopping bag?"

She opened the bag, and inside I saw all of the clothing that she wanted to steal. Somehow, Gypsy convinced the guard to set her free with the merchandise.

"I make deals," she said. "I don't wait for a deal to fall into my lap from another person. See, I'm smart too."

I didn't have any response. The only response that I heard from her was that Gypsy gave the security guard a blow-job in one of the back offices. I shouldn't have asked her, but Gypsy, I could tell, was actually relieved by telling me this. Even though I had grown up in New Hampshire for most of my life, she also had knowledge and a brain, just like all of those New England white girls. I remembered that they still served milk in Albany too.

"You're one of those rich estate boys. Y'know, golden parachutes, nice houses, a trust fund."

"I don't have anything like that. Why do you insist on making me out to be some tycoon, when I'm really not?"

"Stop insulting my intelligence, Charlie," she said, and when she said this, it usually meant that it was time to wrestle her when we returned to my apartment.

"I just can't fathom you and the security officer. What you did is what's wrong with the world. You and that officer - that's what's wrong with the world, and people let it slide almost every day."

"Oh, are you jealous?" she said, batting her eyelashes.

"This is not a game. I am not jealous. All I'm doing is steering myself away from a life of crime with the likes of you. I don't want to be involved in your criminal methods, and I definitely don't want your crack pipes in my bathroom. In fact, when I get home, I'll be the one using the bathroom first. You can use the kitchen sink if you want to wash your hair."

I tried to open the door in such a way that I would be the first one in the bathroom instead of her all the time. I opened it carefully, and when we both saw a one-second vacancy, Gypsy slid in under my arm, ran to the bathroom and then slammed the door shut.

"Dammit, Gypsy, I want you out of here! I want you to leave the apartment! You are a bully, and I don't want to wrestle you anymore, understood?! You don't care about me or anyone else! All you want is your money! Well, sweetheart, I'm not giving you a dime. After you come out, I want you out of here, or else I'm calling the cops!"

Still, no answer. I called the cops to come over. They showed up in a matter of ten minutes. Gypsy came out after I had called the police. Surprisingly she looked really good - the way she dressed and combed her hair. This wasn't the scrawny, flat-chested woman that I met a few months ago. This went beyond a shower. And then the police showed up.

"I lost my twenty dollars," said Gypsy to the Officer.

"Oh, not this again," I said. You haven't lost a thin penny.

Officers, can you please escort this woman away from the premises."

"I can't leave without my twenty dollars," she said to the Officer, "and he claims that he doesn't have it, which is false. I'm sure he has it somewhere."

And then the cop turned to me and said, "Listen, it's obvious she's on something. This area has been quiet all week, and we don't want to cause a fuss. Is there any way you can go to the ATM and get her the twenty dollars?"

Again, she pulls the same type of shit. I never had that twenty dollars earlier, and I still don't have that twenty dollars now. I've never had it. Yet, the outcome was the same. I had to go to the ATM and pay her twenty dollars again. This woman was an unkind thief.

Even though the route to jail or death is the place most addicts fall into, there was something within me that didn't want Gypsy to get stuck in jail. I don't know what caused me to feel this way about her, but as I look back on it now, I can see that I loved this woman, if there were such a thing as love, and also I didn't want to depart from the idea of keeping her safe, protected, and warm. I became the problem.

Not Gypsy. I had to change. I had to open up and ponder the subject of tough love, as this was the last resort. In order to stop her from smoking all of that crack, she had to go to jail just to clean herself up. She woke up in the afternoon and vanished from my apartment with what little money I had left. I didn't want to see her again, though. She had too many problems, and my funds were again so low, that I couldn't possibly see her again.

Some people say that if you are tricked once, it is the other person's fault. Tricked twice, and the fault is yours. I tend to agree with that, but Gypsy became this exception to the rule, and I still don't know why. I figured that I was never capable of love, or maybe I had been capable of it at one time but tucked it deep inside. I just wanted looks to satisfy lusts, and I hope I'm not preaching to the choir here that such relationships, based on lust, won't ever work. I would say that my relationship with Gypsy started off as a lustful one, but suddenly, I wake up in the morning to see her lying there, and I want to care for her, as though she were a wounded animal. To this day, I still don't know what love is, but Gypsy came dangerously close to it.

Chapter Three

I had a couple of days off from the junkyard, and I returned quickly to New Hampshire, because I needed to talk to my father. I needed to convince him that I deserved emergency funds. I was in so much debt with Cash, that I just had to pay him back, and even though my father's hardline stance against money still reigned true, I at least had to try. I even went to New Hampshire with Cash's full blessing. Because of me, Cash was also near to being broke. Both Gypsy and Cash sent me off like I was embarking on some kind of quest, and that one day I would return to save them with good fortune.

I arrived on a Saturday afternoon. Compared to the harsh winters we usually had during that time of year, a lovely and gorgeous spring popped its head up for once. I came off the bus like a businessman wanting to do some important business work for the State of New Hampshire.

My father picked me up from the bus station. He drove a Cadillac SUV, and once inside, I remembered how well I had been cared for as a child, and looking through the windows at the land peeling back, I reconnected to the luxuries and perks of being young and foolishly wealthy.

"How do you like it?"

"What?"

"My new car. It's a Cadillac. In the family we only buy

American cars. We don't prefer those fancy European cars."

"I've noticed."

"What are you driving these days."

"A Ford pickup, mostly for the metal."

"Well, if it's American-made, that works for us. Welcome back to New Hampshire, my dear son. Your mother and I have been concerned about you. We never get phone calls from you anymore.

I'm sure we have a lot of talking to do."

"Yes, Dad."

"Perhaps over dinner. Mom has made pot roast. It's your favorite."

"Thanks, Dad."

He seemed so much kinder than before. Maybe he and Mom really did miss me after I had left for Albany. At this rate, I would wind up in Canada if I followed the towns and cities that were the cheapest. The only way to go was north, even though what I really wanted was to head south, say Mexico City or Costa Rica. Somehow, I am really sensitive to the cold, and I can't stand the harsh Albany winters, even though I was born and raised in New Hampshire. But I still loved New Hampshire. I could tell that things became expensive over time, but I still wanted to sleep in my old bed.

The junkyard job chewed on my bones down in Albany after a while, but as long as I had the job, I could live in my studio there and do work for the junk-man who's payday ruled our lives. I wanted my parents, especially my father, to recognize that I didn't have a future, and that an occasional allowance would help this condition. It was a tough sell.

We sat down for dinner in our family's old dining room. Pictures of my brothers and sisters lined the shelves. I was the only pain in the ass left, and no, I still didn't want to go to college and finish what I had started. I needed access to the green that my mother and father had.

"From what I can tell," said my father during some apple pie, "you aren't doing that well. You have lost a lot of weight. Are you on some kind of diet?"

"With the money I make, I can afford only one large meal in the morning."

"It astonishes me. An Exeter man too. We gave you the option of finishing college, and now you're some kind of junk trader in the middle of nowhere."

"Trinity alums are survivors, and that is what I'm doing. I'm surviving. I don't need a degree for that." "But you're not even an alumnus. Have you thought about a vocational school down there? I don't think you'll go very far collecting junk for a living."

"I don't collect junk, Dad. I haul it away and distribute them through a junkyard."

"What would your fellow Exeter grads say about the job you're doing?"

"I had a few friends at Exeter, and since their families provided them with a everything they've ever wanted for all of their entire lives, I'm sure they're living happily and don't care about the stuff I do."

"Have you learned your lesson about the real world, then? Are you ready to go back to college?"

I felt drowsy and sleepy. At dinner, I could hardly keep my eyes open. I was surprised how I stayed awake. I could do nothing but kiss my mother for the meal she prepared, and I headed up to my room.

I liked being alone in my room after dinner. I had to leave in a couple of days, and the soothing and easy job of relaxing in a familiar place only calmed me. But for my second visit to New Hampshire, my Dad brought up the topic of my new survivor's life, and I would have to keep on pushing the money issue that entire weekend until he agreed to let me into to his high-class wallet. I could easily tell that he wanted me to return to Hartford. I didn't want to, though.

There were no degrees for what I had learned thus far anywhere in the Ivory Tower. I had to tell him about Gypsy as well.

"I have no plans of going back to school, Dad. I'm not reading things like I used to. I'm not intellectually engaged in anything. I want to be a simple man with simple tasks to do, and simple pleasures. I can do a lot, but I won't make much money doing it."

"And you don't mind that?" he asked.

"I do mind it. Nothing I do in life from this point on will make enough money to live like you guys have. I'm broke all the time, and

I also have to help take care of the girlfriend that I have in Albany."

"Why didn't you tell us that you have a girlfriend? That's big news for us. What kind of woman is she?"

"Well, she's not exactly a woman who comes from our world, but I have become fond of her, and I have been seeing her for several months now."

"What does she do?"

"She's into engineering."

"What kind?"

"Mechanical Engineering."

"That's mighty good luck, son. It's amazing that you found a bona-fide engineer where you live."

"She works for the state, so they keep her busy."

"Well, son, all of this is over, okay? We want you to meet a young woman whom we know."

"Oh, Dad, don't match-make for me. I am fine with the woman I just met. Her name is Gypsy."

"That's her name?"

"Yes. Again, I have a very simple life. It's a lot of hard work, but since we talked last time, I have grown used to it. My mind and body have been conditioned this way. This is no time to bring in someone else."

"You do want to be a part of this family, right?"

"Of course, I do."

"Then you'll meet this woman we know. She's a successful

Harvard-educated lawyer."

"I don't need to be matched up by you."

"All I'm asking is for one date," said my father. "Just one date, and if you don't like her, you don't have to see her again."

"One date?"

"Yes. So, let's make plans for you to come up next weekend."

"What about my job? I'm due at work this coming weekend." "All of that is over," said my father.

He pulled out a wad of cash from his pocket and gave it to me.

"Take this for the week. This should be enough."

"Thanks, Dad. But it's only one date, right?"

"You got it. One date."

When he forked over that wad of one-hundreds, I realized that my whole junkyard experience was his way of testing me out. If I had stayed on, it basically meant that he would disown me, but if presented me with a life of more money and re-entrance into the life of wealth and status, it did mean that my junkyard days were over. I jumped at the chance to be a part of the family again. And all I would have to do is date this unknown woman just this one time.

When I returned to Albany, I paid back Cash in full. In a world of such dishonesty, I wanted to give Cash what I owed him. It felt good that I paid him back, because he was shocked that I did so. He was even more shocked that my family wanted me back. But I made him happy, and that is what counted. I also took him out to the Chinese dinner buffet on the outskirts of Albany. He appreciated it. But when I returned to my apartment, for some strange reason, I still wanted to see Gypsy.

After the last workday of hauling junk away, I called her, and within a couple of hours, she came over. She came over in the wee hours of the morning, just before I abandoned the idea of seeing her altogether.

She looked good, even for her scrawny body. I tried to judge if she had lost weight, but I couldn't tell. She seemed hurried, as though she had been rushing to see me. I gave her some of the family money that my father had given me, and she went outside to pay the driver. She returned more relaxed, her face beaming, now that she paid off the driver and scored some crack cocaine off of him. This time she didn't lock herself in my bathroom. She basically pulled out her black-stained glass pipe and smoked the crack right in front of me. Her crack smoking terrorized me, but it also made me happy, because she was happy after sucking down the first few hits for herself. She even offered me a hit, but crack smoking wasn't something I wanted to get into. I was the type of young man who would fall addicted to anything remotely pleasurable. In this case, I watched her smoke it. She then laid back in my bed.

"Gypsy, have you ever thought about getting married?"

She laughed at first, and then said, "no."

"Have you ever fallen in love before?"

"I still don't know what love is, Charlie. Out of many tough things in this world, the trouble is not knowing when love strikes. It can be right away, or it takes time."

"But you've never fallen in love? There wasn't one kid in high school that you really liked?"

"They liked me, and then they eventually found their way to fucking me."

"You're not answering the question, Gypsy."

"Are you asking me to marry you?"

"No. I can't marry you, Gypsy."

"Why not? I'm not pretty enough?" as she batted her eyelashes again and smiled.

"That has nothing to do with it. You live in another world - the street world. You have problems with the law every month, you're a sex worker, you are thief, and you're a crack addict. But most of all, when I ask you for money to borrow, you won't even give me a single penny."

"That's a man's job. To fund women."

"You can't live all your life like that. Men will stay away from you if all you're looking for is money."

"You have to pay up when you're married anyway. What I do cuts through the bullshit and makes love a simple exchange of paying and then fucking. That's how I make my living. I've been at this game for that long."

"If you asked me, I think you have been at this game all your life. Something's buried in you, Gypsy, and it's going to have to come out."

"And you're the rope lassoed around my heart, is that it?"

"No. If you want to be with me, you have to stop the crack, stop the stealing, and get a good job, so that you can survive on your own."

"That's obviously something a father would say."

"Well, can you do that?"

"No. But I bet you still want to get married, right?" "I can't," I said.

"Why not?"

"I'm concerned that my family will disown me. Also, I can't take you back to my town in New Hampshire. They're the type of people who take Christmas seriously."

"You're ashamed of me, then?"

"Just as much as you are ashamed of me, when we walk down to the store on the corner. Whenever those gangsters are out there, gathering at the store, you turn into a different person, and you treat me like I'm a nerd, and then you dive right into a street accent, just to show that you are one of them."

"We're both ashamed of each other," said Gypsy. "Maybe that's why I feel like marrying you. We can go away from here and try something new."

"We can't afford to be together," I said. "I mean, if my parents knew what section of Albany I'm living in, they'd be plenty pissed off. I can't let that happen."

"Because they have all the money? It's obvious that you're loaded."

"I'm not loaded. My parents are. There's a huge difference. And let's stop talking about money all the time. I'm sick about money."

"Y'know, it's funny, because the people who are damn sick of having money on their minds are the ones who are filthy rich. Don't insult my intelligence, Charlie. You think I'm a fool?"

"I do not. I'm just trying to think what marrying you would be like. I can't say that I like the picture. All you do is take, and you never give back. You, my street-walking beauty, don't know what love is yet, and if you don't find out soon, you'll be stuck here."

"Thanks for the warning. I guess you don't want to marry me anymore?"

"I can't Gypsy. I can't have you and the rest of my family at the same time. You now know that."

We both lay in the silence of the early morning. I had work, and this time, she left the apartment when I left. Progress. But at the same time, I did want to marry her, but what would my parents think? I knew that this woman my

141

Dad wanted to meet, this Harvard-educated lawyer, also had a milk-white, dairy smooth upbringing. After a short week at the junkyard, I had to get back to New Hampshire to meet this woman.

I just knew that he had this match planned for a while now, and if it didn't work, I would be sent back to Albany emptyhanded, never to be heard from again.

On the bus ride back up there, I could only think of Gypsy. It was now or never, and I didn't make a decision on it yet, even though I hadn't even met the girl. I relied on God to decide for me. There was little question that I needed some family money. I would ask my father for a lot this time, assuming that this matching plan worked. This dithering, this back-and-forth, this ying-and-yang, this binary circumstance held me by the throat. I didn't care to make the decision. In fact, I had learned over the years that I made terrible decisions. That's when my Dad turned the boat around and let me onto his yacht. At least for a little while.

When I returned to my family's place in New Hampshire, I had been set up to meet this woman. A blind date. Meeting another woman Gypsy's place might have ended this blindly as well.

My mother carefully laid out what I should wear for the evening. Across my bed, she lay a blue blazer, a pin-striped

Oxford shirt, gray woolen pants, and a blue silk tie with matching handkerchief. I hadn't worn clothes like these for some time. In the shower, I scrubbed hard and shaved as close as I could, and when I came out, I felt like a new man, as though the shower relieved all of the stresses and the depressions of the past several months.

This is what I usually wore to formal Exeter functions. It felt good to put on the heavier weight of the clothes. I felt like I belonged in New England again, the strange winters that easily blended into spring, the lake where families went to spend time in the summer heat, this same lake that began to shimmer in the area where we lived. I had a pair of buck oxford shoes, and a pair of Polo socks. If the people of Albany ever saw this, they would think that I was some kind of business tycoon or real estate speculator, or even a great independent equities trader.

I combed my hair with a part to the side, made manageable by styling gel. I checked myself in the bathroom mirror. It reflected what I used to look like before I left Exeter and enrolled at Trinity. I couldn't believe my eyes. My parents couldn't believe theirs either. I was thoroughly transformed, and I missed being this way.

Along with directions to her place, my father also gave me the keys to his Cadillac. He didn't even warn me about staying within the speed limit or making sure that I drove carefully and didn't scratch up the new sealant that protected the car from rust, scratches, and erosion. He simply handed me the keys, and off I went to a town called Londonderry, which was closest to my own town.

I loved the feel of the car. I hadn't been surrounded by such luxury in a long time. The heavy car floated over the smooth roads and curves of New Hampshire's slick and thawing roadways. Within the Cadillac, the front dashboard looked like a cockpit to an airplane. Everything was automatic - locks, cruise control, even the front lights that turned on when a sensor detected darkness. I almost wept before I arrived in Londonderry to pick up my date. I parked quietly in front of a stalwart colonial home. I couldn't believe that I actually missed New England life. I rang the doorbell, and an older aged man appeared. I could tell that he was the head of the household, the father of my date.

"Come in. Come in," he said. "It's chilly out there."

I followed him to a leather couch, where we both sat down and got to know to know one another. No matter how far I had roamed out there, I would always be seen and known as a New Englander when I returned to New Hampshire.

"Can I get you a drink, Charlie? We have tonic or beer."

"If you'd permit me, I think I'll have a beer."

"Great! Me too."

After returning with the beer, he sat down across from me on the couch.

"So, Charlie, I hear that you were going to college, but had a change of plan."

"Yes, sir, I did. I wanted to know what the real world was like."

"Really? College wasn't teaching you about that?"

"As far as I'm concerned, college taught me about the intellect, not how to survive and stand on my own two feet."

"Wow! I've never known anyone who has done that before. You must have a real adventurist side to you."

"What do you do for work, sir? If you don't mind my asking."

"I'm an investment banker. Worked in it for most of my life thus far."

"That sounds great to me," I said, sipping my beer and trying not to gulp it down as fast as I could.

"Yes, we've been lucky, thank God. But do you plan to go back to college?"

"Not just yet, but soon."

"What do you do for work, then?"

"I'm in Waste management. I've been doing it for almost a year now."

"Well, I would prefer my daughter go out with someone with a bachelor's degree."

"I understand that, sir, but I'm doing well out in Albany."

"Still. An education is always something you can fall back on. It's something that no one can ever take away from you. My daughter just recently graduated from Harvard Law, and she's ready for the world too. A few law firms are interested in hiring her."

"That sounds great. You must be very proud."

"Yes, our daughter does us proud. She's been like that since her childhood. She always tried to help us, the parents. Can you believe that? My young girl requesting that she run the household at age fourteen?"

"Yes, a very precocious daughter. It will be an honor to have dinner with her tonight."

"In fact, let me go see if she's ready."

The father went to the foot of the stairwell to the second floor of the house and called her name a few times.

"Mildred! Your date is waiting for you down here."

"Okay, Dad!" came a voice from upstairs. "Just a few more minutes."

The father then returned to his same seat, and within a few moments, a wonderful young woman in a pink dress descended the stairs. She had brown hair and blue eyes, and the dress she wore looked wonderful on her. I originally thought that this woman was going to be an ugly nerdish kind of like I was in college, but I was dead wrong. When I saw her, I breathed a huge sigh of relief. She looked a lot better than I thought she'd look. Once again, my father came through. He came up with a rescue plan, and Mildred, in this case, became the rescue plan.

I immediately wanted for us to get out of the house and visit the restaurant in downtown Londonderry. The place downtown served gourmet meals, and I thought it the perfect place to take Mildred. But when we loaded ourselves into the Cadillac and drove into town, she said that she didn't want to go to the restaurant that I picked out. Instead, she wanted to go to a vegan salad place not too far from the town's border. How could I ignore such a request? If she ate salad, I'd eat salad too. I didn't think it a big deal.

We drove to the salad place. It was cramped and small but crowded and bustling with business. We looked ridiculous in our dress, though. But the place, apparently, was expensive and fashionable. People waited in the lobby for a chance to get a seat. We were terribly overdressed for such a place, though. Mildred and I waited, but apparently, she knew everyone in the place. Even though the others on line groaned that a table wasn't available yet, we were ushered right to a table with a nice view of a small creek that roamed through the restaurant's back yard.

I wondered, then, how many people Mildred knew. She even knew the name of her waitress, as though they had been best friends for years. I guess with a degree from Harvard Law, one really does have to sacrifice oneself for the town every now and then. While the restaurant partook in the crunch of lettuce and croutons, it was easy to see that Mildred couldn't have made it into Harvard alone, but with her community helping her as well. It was refreshing to see.

I ordered the grilled chicken Caesar salad. She ordered the chef's salad. I was actually eating healthy for a change. In Albany, the main meal every night was a baloney sandwich and a cheap slice of pizza. But now, I was reminded of my old acquaintances in the area, and how they were getting ahead, taking care of children and such, and doing very well at it. I also recognized a few of the townsfolk on my way into the restaurant. Everyone looked clean and healthy, while I felt dogged and fatigued. With my best jacket and tie on, they must of thought that here's a person working at some corporation that was too big to fail, and that I too was doing well, with this stunning-looking woman sitting across from me having a massive Chef's salad.

"Your father and my father are very good friends," she said, stabbing at a tomato in her salad. "They worked together for a while in Boston, I think."

"Yeah. My father is a really great guy, and I'm sure your father is too."

"And you're in Albany, New York, right now? I've never been there myself, so I don't know what it's like."

"Oh, I love Albany, but the weather is terrible. The winter pushes an Arctic wind coming down from Canada. But other than the cold winters, everything is great."

"And you're in the waste disposal business?"

"Yep, that's me."

"I'm due to return to Boston next Fall. I've decided to take a position as a lawyer there at a good law firm."

"Good for you. I guess you have the summer off to prepare."

"Yes," she said. "I really want to do some traveling. Hopefully to South America."

"Really? Wow. Which part?"

"Brasilia. I may be able to make it there for free through Harvard. An international corporate law firm there is already interested in bringing me on as a partner."

"But you haven't even finished law school yet."

"I guess it's one of the perks of going to Harvard Law."

"It's an amazing time for you. Grab it and make it last for as long as you can. I'm sure South America would love to have you."

"Awww. That's so sweet of you."

"Just stating the facts. You're a woman of the world. Now is the time to make it happen, because when you're older, well…"

"What happens when we're older?"

"We kind of get, well, reset. You know what I mean?"

"Not really, no."

"Let me put it this way. Things start slowing down, and those same opportunities are not available. I look at it as being brainwashed by some higher entity."

"Excuse me?"

"It's kind of like being brainwashed by celestial spirits or space aliens. I know it sounds weird, but it's true. The mind shrinks. One specializes in one's own life. There are only a few things a man can do, and that's to make a lot of money and get laid as often as possible."

"I don't understand," she said, looking down at her salad.

"You'll figure it out, but if you don't grow older by the time these aliens do their review, they'll throw you out."

"That's an interesting theory, Charlie."

"See! That's all by design. It's predetermined that we belong to what either the spirits or what the aliens want from us. Of course, we have choices. It depends on what you believe in. But overall, it seems as though you've been selected - like a queen warrior almost, like that television show - Sheena, the Animal Woman, I think it was called."

"I've never heard anything like…"

"I'm just getting started. You see, I have discovered that we are among aliens, especially people who are very well-educated and rise right to the top of the ladder, if you know what I mean. I myself am on the list. We're talking aliens who beam down upon this Earth and then take control of the minds of the less talented ones. I am one of those aliens, Mildred. Really, I am! You may be one of them but only the aliens can tell, when they communicate to their selectees.

"Anyway," I continued, "what we do is, right, is we rise right to the top, and then after a short time, we are able to control their minds through sonic waves that come straight out of our foreheads…"

"Charlie, you're making me a little uncomfortable."

"Just wait! So, once we take control of their minds, we direct them towards secret sex houses."

"Gee, Charlie, it is getting kind of late."

151

"Just listen! Anyway, once they're in this alien sex houses, we strip them, from head to toe – the male aliens strip the human females, and the female aliens strip the male humans. The aliens then fuck the shit out of the humans. Right then and there!"

"Charlie, please. You're making a scene."

"Just let me finish, please! I gave you time, now you give me some fucking time! What I have to tell you is vitally important to our alien species and to you too, because you may not be selected yet. As I was saying, we really fuck the shit out of the humans, and right then and there, our beautiful alien offspring drop onto the floor of the sex house. For the human men, it comes out of their rectums. For the female humans, it comes out of there, well, you know."

"I really have to get going now, Charlie. You really need to take me home."

"Why? It's only seven in the evening."

"I have to get up early."

"But at least finish your salad. There's still a lot on your plate, and there's a lot to tell you about how I developed these theories."

"I really do have to get home, Charlie."

"And then, soon after the alien offspring drop, we kidnap them and take them to our transporter. And you know what happens after that?"

"Sir, you would like the check?" asked the waiter forcefully.

"No, not yet!. Anyway," he continued, "we eat the body parts – the afterbirth, the womb, the intestines, all of it - piece by piece, of the humans we just impregnated. And then, we are let out again, looking for more people. You just better watch yourself. Make sure you do well down in Brasilia, and they'll come to you and instead of you being forced into them!"

"But I insist, sir," said the waiter.

"You're ridiculous!" she said, throwing down the linen napkin she wiped her mouth with.

When I drove her home, she bid me a quiet goodnight and almost ran to the front door where her father let her in. It would be the last I would see of her, because when I went back to my parent's house and awoke the next day, I found my father sitting next to me on my bed.

"Space aliens, Charlie? What the hell was that all about? You basically told her that we're being invaded by space aliens or some other bullshit that you thought up?"

"Good morning to you too, Dad," I groaned. "I guess the date didn't go as planned."

"No. You threw that whole date on purpose, didn't you? Because if you didn't, I'm calling the doctor."

"It wasn't on purpose. I just wanted to expose how daunting getting older could feel like."

"Oh, Charlie. What are we supposed to do with you? You block our every move. Don't lie and say that you actually think that. You wanted out. Admit it."

I rolled over and propped myself on my arm. My father, besides being tough and angry, now seemed a little depressed that one of his sons just didn't get it.

"You should get back to Albany today. I'm too stressed out and worried to have you stay. We give you the chance of a good life, and suddenly, you pull this shit."

"I'm sorry, Dad, but I just don't want to be around that crowd."

"Oh, I see. You mean the ones who do well in school and come out of there and get good jobs and live happy lives? Instead, you trade it in for something that you're having with this engineer friend of yours?"

"I'm sorry, Dad, but maybe it wasn't meant to be with this lawyer. At least I have that SUNY mechanical engineer in Albany that I still date. Isn't that enough?"

"Oh, no," he sighed. "A SUNY mechanical engineer? I just don't know about you anymore, son. Did you get her pregnant too? I just don't know anymore."

His hand massaged his brow and the stubble around his mighty Hemingway face. He was clearly disappointed, and I couldn't really do anything about it. He told me that he would drop me off at the bus station headed to Albany that morning. I would be on my own, even though both of us didn't like the idea. It was tough love all over again, that 'cruel to be kind' lesson that he was teaching me. He wanted me in the family, but he didn't want to risk the whole yacht for the rudderless raft that I represented.

"I'm sorry, Dad. The last person I wanted to disappoint was you."

"I know that, son. It just doesn't seem that way. We send you to Exeter, then Trinity, and in the end, you're just living life on the loose in Albany. You need a good job, and you need to get going. I'm sorry."

My Dad, being the sweet and caring man, he had always been, had no choice but to furnish me with another wad of cash before sending me on my way. I knew that I wouldn't be able to see him for a long time. I had my chances, and I didn't take them. The responsibility was all mine, and as I rode on the bus, I owned that responsibility. I didn't want to go to school, and I didn't want that Harvard Law grad either. Actually, what I wanted to do was call Gypsy as soon as I got home and also place a call to Cash. We were all even in terms of money, so I wouldn't have to bum off of him for a long while. I could just continue where I left off, which is exactly what I did.

Returning to Albany, though, had a happy effect on me. To see the Empire State towers, the odd-shaped Egg, even some of the abandoned buildings and industrial plants at the edge of the Hudson gave me an incredible sense of freedom. Sure, there was no money, but if there ever were a place that I thought I could live without money, it had to be Albany. The small city made belonging available to a man with any kind of income.

I took some of the money my father gave me, and I called Gypsy as soon as I dropped my bag on the apartment floor when I finally arrived home.

Instead of going right for the bathroom, this time she went straight to my bed, sucked in the crack cocaine that she had, pulled off her skimpy dress, and slid under my cool bed sheets.

"I've missed you too," she said, moving from crack pipe to cigarette.

We first made love. Our conversation came second.

"So, you go to see your wealthy family?" she asked.

"They're not wealthy, but yes, I saw my wealthy family. They set me up with a date."

"And, I take it, you like her better than you like me?"

"Actually, it's the other way around," I said.

"Now Charlie, why did you make such a bad decision? You don't want someone like me. I'm a just a street 'ho."

"They call it 'sex worker' nowadays," I said, "and you're my girlfriend."

"That's what I wanted to make clear to you, Charlie. I am not your girlfriend."

"But we've been going together ever since I moved to Albany. We've been seeing each other for a while now, and I see you often, which must mean that I am your boyfriend."

We sat up in bed in the nighttime din of ambulance sirens, fire truck horns, and police lights as they rushed down the street right next to my apartment. I wanted this to work between us, but Gypsy was so resolute about being a single prostitute that I had the misfortune of asking, "haven't you ever wanted to be something more than a sex worker?"

"I was rich before I got here too, y'know."

"What do you mean?"

"I used to have loads of money too, but I burned through it. I was living all the way up."

"What was it that knocked you down?"

"I had my daughter."

"You?"

"Yes, even me. A lot of us 'hoes are single mothers with derelict fathers who run out or we never hear from again. My mother has custody over her, because I pull in a lot of money off the streets. After my daughter was born, though, I had to slow things down, and now I barely make what I used to make."

"But what did you want to be when you were growing up?"

"I wanted to be a cosmetologist. I wanted to go to beauty school. Such schools are too expensive. And I guess now you don't want me as your girlfriend, I take it."

"Actually, the opposite is true, but I understand the futility of it. We're not getting any younger, Gypsy. We have to do something that we can live off of."

"That's the problem, Charlie. Who wants a minimum wage job when one can deal crack or sell themselves on the side?"

I understood that this happened to be the real tragedy - not enough high-paying jobs and the resulting crime that littered the streets. I had been roped into it as well. I would have to work three jobs to able to afford a larger apartment or one of those bottom-shelf Korean cars that zipped around these streets and caused so much mayhem. I could easily tell when the new convenience stores selling crack and heroin opened up on the corners of this section of the city.

The world that both Gypsy and I inhabited, then, were stunningly the same. We landed in the same positions, the only difference being that she had a crack addiction, almost like an under-appreciated war veteran, and myself, just by being around the crack and heroin-addicted, rubbed her poverty off on me, as though I were in their same class, now that Dad wouldn't take me back. While I still had some upper-class pride, I couldn't deny that such a class heritage doesn't automatically make one higher or lower than anybody else. This is what I had turned into, and if this was to be the start of a new life, it had to be with Gypsy. I wanted to marry her.

"Why would you want to marry me, Charlie? I'm a crack-addicted hooker. What would your family say?"

"I am independent of my family," I said. "I do want to marry you. We've both fallen way down, Gypsy, and once we have fallen down through the view of any society, not only ours, there's no way back. You are the angel that God has left for me at this terrible level, and only together can we pull ourselves out of this abyss. I'm willing to try if you are."

She chuckled, and said, "God, Charlie, you are so stupid. You know nothing about what goes around here."

"Yeah, but I'm starting to learn, and if this is a coupling that the Lord has given us, then I say we take advantage of it."

She rolled over and kissed me. She ran her fingers through my hair.

"Charlie, I can't marry you, if that's what you want. I'm too far gone, Charlie. You can't reel me in like this. I know you're in love with me, but I just don't want to get married."

I fell asleep that night with the woman I wanted to marry, and when I woke up early in the morning ready for work, she had gone. I called her name through my dingy, dark apartment, but no one was there. I tried calling her cell phone, just to make sure she got home okay, but there was no answer.

I went to work early, because I wanted some advice from Cash. He arrived right on time for work, and after talking with the boss-man for a little bit, I caught him on the way out of the junkyard.

"Jeez, Charlie, I don't know what to say. I know I hooked you guys up, and maybe you'd see each other for a few days, but marriage? To Gypsy?"

"What's so wrong with that?"

"She's a hooker, Charlie, who has tricked you to such an extent that you actually fell in love with her. You see?

You're her dream client. Please, man, will you, please. Don't call her again. If you two were married, you would fall right down the tubes with her. You'd be just another junkie in Albany. I don't want to see that happen to you, Charlie. You are a good, strong man. You taught me how to do this crummy job, and for that I'll always be thankful. It's obvious to me that you are one of the smartest people I've met too. You fell from the big castle tower. Don't be foolish by hanging around her anymore. You need to break free of her. If I would have known you'd fall in love with her, I would have never introduced you two in the first place. Damn. I never saw it coming, and I'm so sorry I hooked you guys up to begin with."

"I think I'm in love with her, Cash."

"Oh, boy," said Cash, "Let's go out after work, then. We can have a few beers and talk it over. But until you see me tonight, do not call her. Don't even think about it, okay? You're in love with a prostitute, Charlie. We need to flesh this out a little more."

I called Gypsy before I met Cash at the bar, but again, all I got was her voicemail and the annoying computerized message that said her voicemail was full. I tried her several times until I realized what I dope I was being.

The next day, I was at work, and I wasn't at work. I could only think of Gypsy. Thoughts of our marriage

161

became the blurry line of thinking too much about her and then hauling light pieces of junk away from the sidewalks. It was somewhat of a day off, and the boss-man saw right through it. I left early and headed for the bar where Cash and I hung out for the second night in a row. He said he still needed to talk some sense into me. I hoped he could steer me in the right direction. When he finally arrived, I ordered a round of beer for the both of us. I made it clear that I would be paying the bar tab tonight.

There were several widescreen televisions at the bar displaying soccer games from Europe, also a couple of baseball games, now that spring had finally arrived. I didn't feel like drinking at all, but I thought that I deserved to have one night of a drunken binge, and

Cash would be there to drive me home. I hope I wasn't leaning on Cash too much. He had done many good things for me, and I wanted to show my appreciation by having this man-to-man drunk-fest over the damaged women in our lives.

I could tell that Cash had had plenty of relationships with Albany women, and they all turned to shit. He blamed the women for wanting too much, and they blamed him, because they thought that he was too tightfisted and, overall, too concerned about doing the right thing all the time. I didn't blame Cash. Poverty does suck. They were right

162

when they had made those old posters. People just liked having the security of money and what it could bring them.

Cash knew how to protect his money, while I easily buckled under the pressure of giving Gypsy too much. Yet I still wanted the country home and the Volvo in the garage. Actually, I began thinking of my simple suburban dream as puerile. There would be no suburbia for me. It would be the 'hood, twenty-four-seven. All of that dreaming seemed to be over, and I found myself at ground-zero, exactly where I started, getting drunk as usual. The server led us out of the bar area and to a table near hungry patrons who somehow ate all of their gigantic portions.

"I don't know what the hell to do with you, Charlie. We get separated from working together, and then everything turns to chaos. I introduce you to a woman and suddenly you want to marry her. Charlie, you're playing with fire. I never expected for things to get this out of hand." "It's not exactly a bad thing," I said.

"You make it sound like a terrible mistake when it isn't."

"You know better," said Cash. "Did you tell your family about this?"

"I told them that I was dating a successful Harvard engineer. I don't think they believed me. They set me up with someone else."

"And?"

"I just couldn't do it. I thought about Gypsy the whole time."

"Absence makes the heart forget. Maybe you should leave town for a little while, so you won't have to see her anymore."

"I'll be in a lot of pain if I do that."

"Feeling pain is much better than marrying Gypsy, that's for sure. Listen, you can't see what a big mistake you're making. Other people can, but you are too swayed by your emotions for her that you are no longer thinking rationally. This woman is trouble, Charlie. You can't see her anymore. Otherwise, you'll destroy your life and your family's life."

"People don't know I feel."

"I, for one, do know how you feel. Cut her loose, feel like shit for a few days, and go back to New Hampshire. And ask your father to hook you up again. That's the answer. You need to see how foolish you are by wanting to marry her. Hell, sometimes I blame myself."

"You're not at fault for this in any way shape, shape, or form. Don't do that to yourself. You never thought that I'd fall for her. I never thought so either, but over time, we met at some middle ground, where she is more open to the idea of marriage than ever before. She is at least considering the idea."

"Great. That's just great. She's a fucking prostitute, Charlie!"

"Whatever you want to call her - prostitute, whore, sex worker, sex healer, woman of the night, all women like these deserve to find love in their lives too. They deserve to be loved. I just don't see why marrying a prostitute is such a problem."

We ordered another round. The beer was mild, light, and refreshing. Cash had grown frustrated with our conversation, but he stayed with me until I got completely plastered. I had no other way home, and Cash drove me. My lips slurred some further talk about Gypsy before I passed out in the passenger seat of his truck. When I got home, Cash hoisted me up from the passenger's seat, and with my arm slung over his shoulder, he dragged me to my apartment. He dropped me on the bed and covered me with a blanket. That's all I can remember of that evening.

I skipped work the next day. I was too hungover to do any kind of hauling. It was then, as I lay in bed recovering, that my boss called from the junkyard. He fired me for having too many absences and being late one too many times. Such a sentence didn't wake me up, though. I fell back into bed until it was almost nine at night. I called Cash right away when I awoke.

"Maybe this wasn't the right kind of work for you." "I liked it, though," I said.

"Regardless, Charlie, we all pushed hard for you, but the Boss-man always has the right of way. And now that you've disentangled yourself from the junkyard, you need to find work right away - and we're talking minimum-wage work at a coffee shop or restaurant. Maybe washing dishes until you can make it back on top."

"I've never been at the top, Cash."

"You know, and I know, that you were born at the top, and like the big, sacred Buddha, you fell to the earth, right on top of that fucking junkyard. You have to use whatever you have. You've got to use it to finagle your way back into white culture and society, or else, Charlie, you're never going to make it back. My cousin tried to do the same thing, except that he wanted to be a hip-hop star. So, he hung out, or at least tried to hang out, at places where hip-hop took control - we're talking bars and bodegas."

"And what happened to him?"

"He never had the talent. He was behind the scenes as a lyricist and a producer. And now he's sitting pretty in Malibu, California somewhere. He made it to the top, and you will too. I know you will. Hell, you even look and sound

166

like gentry. You don't need me anymore. You need some connections who know about you and how smart you are."

"I don't feel very smart right now. I never had many friends."

"That's what you need. You need a bar - not to drink - but to hang out with some wealthy people, so that they can find you a good job."

"What about Gypsy?"

"Man, I'm not going to say this again. Get rid of her. She takes your money and gets a free ride. I don't want to hear about Gypsy again, either."

"What about you?"

"You don't need to see me again either. I hate to sound like this, but I think you need to find your own culture. The junkyard is not in your culture. Rising to the top - that's in your genes."

"You've always been very good to me, Cash. How will I survive?"

"Tonight, you go to a bar, the most expensive bar in Albany, and you strike up a conversation with someone. And do not drink! That's another unusual habit you've developed. And dress like you mean it."

I said goodnight to Cash, and I had never felt so vulnerable before than when we both hung up the phone. He didn't want to see me again. We were parting ways, almost like a teacher and his student parting ways. As his figurative student, though, I still wanted to be a part of his life, but this would never work. When I walked the streets of Albany, only the white guys looked like they wanted to know me. The black folk stayed away.

When a new, nauseous-free, sunny day had arrived, I looked through all of the clothing that I had. I chose the best shirt and pants that I had. I had put these clothes away, because I never thought that I'd have to use them again, but I guess I was wrong about that too. I made many mistakes, and my mistakes were my own. No one else's. I still didn't want to go back to college. The decision kept rolling in and out of my mind.

I put on the nice clothes, and in the dirty mirror hanging up in the bathroom, I saw a different person altogether. I slipped on my buck Oxford shoes as well, and for that night, I left my apartment and walked south to where the white people lived.

I wasn't used to the person I rediscovered in the mirror just yet. He looked conniving, mysterious, and I dare say, unwelcome, but we hadn't even reached the bar yet, so I tried to keep my mind wide open and remembered what Cash had told me.

It was an interesting place. I knew exactly where I needed to go. Along the border of Albany and the next town over, Latham, the entrance to a large shopping mall stood beside a crowded route that unfurled into the country. The bar rested on a knoll that had its borders for nightlife clearly demarcated. The patios on each side of the bar let in the cool air. Younger, beautiful women crowded the place as though they had been waiting for a good suitor for the longest of times. Soon, they would get tired and wander away, thinking bars shitty places to meet men. For me? I just liked to look at these women.

I had very little courage to walk up to these women and talk to them back then. They had always arrived with company, and it became difficult to maneuver around their friends and barge into conversations, until, finally, the women wanted me gone. Other men always cock-blocked me. And then I wouldn't stop bothering these starlets and beauty queens, and the final step always involved a couple of bouncers who threw me out.

Luckily this all didn't happen yet, but I made sure not to bother anyone or make fools of them. It became priority number one to behave myself as I sat at the bar and ordered drinks. I must have drunk beer for a couple of hours straight, just one after the other. I loosened up and started to approach women. One of them must have complained, because what were once party havens now proved to be tricky waters to find someone to take home for the night. Bars, apparently, no longer catered to the much desired one-night stands. I had to sit alone and drink until I blacked out. The next thing I knew I was alone in my apartment unsure of how the night ended or how I got home. I just didn't remember. I couldn't remember anything.

I stayed in bed terribly hungover. I was sick and not thinking straight. I regretted even going to the Latham bar, but as the day stretched out, I did get a phone call. It was Gypsy. Her voice and her commitment to coming over that evening made me feel better. I had a little cash left for her. I had to spend it on her. I thought she'd cure my sickness from the night before. All I yearned for my body, my sick, sweating body, melting into her soft skin and her willingness to do whatever I wanted. She treated me much better than any other time before after she undressed, as though I were a frequent flyer or had coupons and frequent flyer miles for the time with spent with her, or a VIP pass of some sort. She must have missed me.

"Do you still want to marry me?" she asked as she got up to have a cigarette after making love to me.

"I'm all out of money, Gypsy. I have nothing left."

"Are you getting a job?"

"It doesn't look good from that angle either."

"I can't come back, Charlie. You would still have to pay for my services, whether you could afford it or not."

"If we got married? What then?"

"Do you really want to marry me? It doesn't seem like you're very serious about it."

"I just don't know anymore. Things have gotten so confusing for me. I don't know anything - what to do, what to wear, who to call. I just feel like sleeping a lot." "Sounds like you're pretty damned depressed," she said.

"Yeah."

"Well, you have a lot to be depressed about. You just lost your job, your family said goodbye to you. Albany is a new place for you, and you want to have a family. I don't know either, Charlie. You've taken a dive. I don't know how to help you."

"You mean you actually want to help me? That's something new."

"Are you still going to work minimum wage?"

"I don't have anything else."

"What if I said that I can show you how to be rich?"

"I'd say, fill me in."

"I have friends who may be in need of some help."

"Doing what?"

"Selling drugs."

I chuckled here, because I had to. This is what my life had boiled down to.

"I'll wind up in jail."

"Maybe, but I think you're missing the point."

"Me? That I'll wind up in jail?"

"Charlie, don't insult my intelligence."

"For the last time, I am not trying to insult your intelligence."

"People are making thousands. If you sell crack or H, you at least have a chance. Tomorrow, I'll take you to some people around here that I know."

"It's already tomorrow. It's three in the morning."

"Sleep then. We'll have the afternoon and evening of tomorrow to get you hooked up, okay? Don't worry so much. Let's see what they say."

"Who's they?"

Chapter Four

Gypsy had always been a fast walker. When we entered the avenue that would take us further into some of the most dangerous streets of the area, I could easily tell that the neighbors that I saw there were totally disenfranchised. Abandoned houses, broken windows, weak and sagging front porches, big red signs on the doors defining houses as abandoned or ready to be wrecked. Even bricks from these houses had fallen from the rooftops and crumbled on the roads and sidewalks, indicating these were once-wonderful houses that fell into the nebula of negligence and disrepair.

As I followed Gypsy, I couldn't understand the reasons why such neighborhoods remained so pock-marked and weak, as though carpet-bombed by the jet planes that flew into the local airport. It was the scenery of a permanent underclass, and I am still unsure, to this date, that anyone could do anything about it.

"Would you come on, Charlie," said Gypsy. "Stop thinking, and start walking."

She slowed down for me and slipped her arm through mine for my tour of the fierce streets where no one seemed to have money. It may have all been hidden in these gutted apartments instead. The 'hood community only bought amazing cars, some of them custom made, but aside from this extravagance, they paid little or no attention to turning these properties around. They were not the owners of these properties, and the landlords didn't care so much about what they did. Only new landlords with the ability to repair properties, with help from the city, could fix up these properties.

People in the 'hood stayed away from that, and one day, the landlords would want them out. The 'hood population would again be displaced and disenfranchised, as wealthier people moved in and made Albany's real estate costs way too high for anyone to afford. For now, though, Gypsy introduced him to the long stretch of street where they had to go.

"Let me do the talking first, okay?" she said, and then she kissed me, as though I were boarding a long roller coaster that I would probably fall from.

We approached one of the nicer brownstones in the neutral zone. It was a place where blacks and whites and Asians, and also students, all lived in party-hardy solidarity. They were still under the burden of pressing economic stress, but they were able to pay rent in better buildings. I easily saw that these neighborhoods started off as black, then mixed, then they turned purely white further south of the small city. We, however, didn't get very far into these white neighborhoods. We remained in the mixed area and walked up to a clean and well-maintained townhouse that had a nice lobby with cherry wood floors.

I followed Gypsy into the darkness of a stained marble lobby and creaking stairs. I had no idea what we were doing, but I just hung on to her, hoping that she would find it. I was shaking all over, still wondering if this was what I should have been doing with my life.

We went up three flights of stairs. There was only one apartment door, which Gypsy knocked on. The guy looked in the eye of his door, and then let us in.

He was a short guy with gold teeth and a brand-new baseball hat without a price tag, but new factory stickers still on its brim. The sight of the man's teeth made me uneasy, but after a few minutes of showing us where to sit and what we'd like to drink, I knew that this man had been taught manners as imposing as those at Exeter. I knew I was in the right territory, and yet I didn't open my mouth. It was Gypsy who talked, because it appeared that the man had been friends with her for quite some time.

"And who's this?" he asked.

"Sorry, how rude," I said. "I'm Charlie, and I am a good friend of Gypsy's. I know you are busy, and your time must be valuable."

"It's okay," he said.

"Charlie wants to get into the game," said Gypsy.

"The game? This guy? I could see him from a mile away. He wouldn't be able to stay out of sight."

"We need it," she said, "but it's all business. Charlie doesn't do drugs, and he would make a lot selling easy to these students and white people. These are territories that we can't go into, but Charlie here, he's perfect for the job. He can blend-in, get his own clients. He's a real money-maker, if you ask me."

"You think so?"

"Yes," said Gypsy, "I do."

"I would like a different crew in the South End. Do you have any experience with this stuff?"

"Only what Gypsy has taught me so far."

"You want to sell heroin or crack?"

"Since Gypsy is into crack," said Charlie, "I thought I'd go into heroin just to make our relationship less of a hassle. She wants nothing to do with heroin, and I don't want anything to do with crack."

"Smart boy," he said, "but we're gonna try you out first."

The man walked over to a rusty file cabinet. He unlocked it and pulled open a drawer. He took out five small bags of heroin.

"You think you could sell five of these by tomorrow?"

"Wow," said Charlie. "I can try."

"The difference between doing and trying is a hole through your head."

"Thanks," said Charlie. "I'll bring back whatever I sell."

"Hold on," they both seemed to say at once.

"You have to pay me first. We don't cuff around here."

"Cuff?"

"You have to pay up front," said Gypsy.

"How much does it cost?"

"We're talking half a bundle, so that's sixty dollars."

"I can do it," said Charlie again, but this time he wasn't so confident. He had little idea that they would kill him for trying new things. But this wasn't college or high school. This was the street, and there were plenty of people who had been shot due to the massive drug trade that existed all throughout New England and most of New York.

"I don't have sixty on me. Would you mind too much if I had a private talk with Gypsy for a second?"
"Go right ahead," said the man.

"Gypsy," I whispered, "I don't have any money for this. Can you, for once, buy this stuff for me, and I'll pay you back."

At first, Gypsy hesitated, but then, after struggling with her own thoughts, came up with a proposition that proved agreeable to us both.

"I'll take half of what you make on this deal. You've got sixty dollars-worth. A half-bundle. That's one-hundred and twenty out on the street. You pay me what you owe me, which is sixty dollars, plus a half of what you make. So, you pay me ninety bucks. The rest you keep."

"Gee, Gypsy. That doesn't leave me with much."

"Stop talking like some kind of nerd, okay? This is how it is for a lot of us. You need to start just like everyone else."

"Fine," said Charlie to the man. "I'll take the half bundle."

Gypsy took out sixty dollars from whatever cleavage she had under her dress and forked it over to Charlie. Charlie then counted it and handed it over to the man. He counted the cash swiftly and gave them the half-bundle of five bags.

"You run out," said the man, "I want you to come right back to me."

And finally, after reassembling our courage, we left the den the man lived in and returned to my apartment. Once there, Gypsy and I made love, took showers, changed our clothes, and soon enough, we were off to find clients for the heroin we just purchased. The showers had relaxed us, as we had plenty of time to think and space out underneath the drumming hot water of the shower. Once we both dressed, we decided that we'd would go to the local Chinese buffet and plan things out over a healthy dinner.

We took a table farther away from the rowdy kids and their equally loud parents. Our meals were a study in contrasts. Gypsy ate nothing but fruit and salad, while I loaded up on every fatty food one could imagine - chicken with peanut sauce, General Tso's chicken, and beef with broccoli. I had a plate full of this, and then went to the buffet again to get the egg rolls, the fried shrimp, and the fried dumplings. By the time I returned for my second plate, Gypsy wanted to talk.

"We have to think about this," she said.

"What's there to think about? We can sell it when we get home."

"Not where you are, Charlie."

"What do you mean?"

"There are gangs in the 'hood that fight for territory. We can't go where they're already selling."

"Why not?"

"Because they'll kill us if we step on their turf."

"Oh. Maybe we should buy some guns?"

"You are such a retard," she said. "We're not going to buy guns. This isn't the Wild West, idiot."

"Then what? Who are we selling to?"

"We have no choice but to hang around the other side of the tracks."

"You mean, the white areas?"

"Yeah," she said. "We have to sell to white people."

"That's an easy arrest for the cops. We'd be thrown in jail the second we step out there."

"It's better than getting killed."

"So, what are you saying? That the real choices in all of this is between going to jail or getting killed?"

"We can do it in a way that makes it work, and this is what I have to explain to you."

"Please do."

"Because you are white, you automatically blend in with them. You look like them and act like them. The 'hood hasn't rubbed off on you yet. You need to make some connections on the white side of town."

"But I don't know anyone on the white side of town," I said nervously.

"That's where we have to start."

She pulled out another forty from her dress.

"Take this," she said, as she handed over forty dollars. "You need to go to the clubs, where they dance, or to a regular bar, where they play music. These are the people you need to sell it to, and if we do sell, we can have at least five clients by the end of the weekend. You shouldn't deal in these clubs. Just stand outside until closing and see what happens."

"What about the cops?"

180

"You'll have to avoid them."

"Where will you be all this time?"

"As far as I know, you now owe me the one-twenty. That's my connection to you. I'm on the outside of this, Charlie. You owe me money now, and if you don't re-up, we're out of business. The man already got what he wanted, which was the sixty we gave him for the half-bundle. Then I get what I want. Then you get to re-up. That's how we move up in the chain. Whoever sells the most gets to talk to the man about future projects, like selling the stuff out of state, stuff like that."

"My God, what have I gotten into. We're talking jail and death."

"It won't be that bad, okay, sweetie. Just take the forty dollars, and sell each bag for twenty or thirty bucks. After you're done, you'll call me on your cell phone, okay? Don't be scared. I know you are, but now is the time to make what we can as fast as we can, and then head down to the Caribbean where no one can find us, at least after we get the trust of the wholesaler we just met. You'll make it. Just show a little confidence and a tiny bit flash. At least I know you can do it. But besides that, you have to look like a true player outside these clubs."

"With forty dollars? That's all you can front me."

"Now you're sounding like a man in the game. You should have a few clients that will come to you, because the man's dope is rumored to be pretty good."

The next part of our plan involved going to the mall, and with clothes that she selected for me, I would become more fashionable to the white party circuit that always ran like a flood through Albany's night-time streets. The clothes were outrageous, and I didn't look genuine wearing them, but Gypsy insisted that I had to look a certain way to gain attraction. She also picked up a couple of dresses for herself, which I had to pay for with what little money I had left.

When we returned home with shopping bags full of new merchandise, I donned mine and walked around the streets with Gypsy.

"But what about you?"

"I'll be there, so you don't have to worry about that."

"I mean, you'll be able to blend in too?"

"Oh. Yes, I'll blend in fine. My skin is mostly white. I've hung out with white people before. I can go both ways, black and white."

"I see."

We found a small bar near the Albany capital of social life, which was Lark Street. All down Lark Street the neon lights were inviting. People who lived on Lark Street were either very wealthy or wanted to lose their minds within the swirl of both hard drugs and alcohol.

The din of each bar spilled out into the street.

I stood outside one of these bars. From what Gypsy told me, no one really did heroin inside the bars or the clubs. I had to wait outside. When I did introduce myself and propositioned them with the heroin on their way in, they were somewhat interested in taking their party to the next heavenly plane, but overall, they were too nervous about it. All of them said no thanks, and I returned back to Gypsy.

"You can't just ask them and go away," she said. "You have to work it, just like any other salesman. You have to almost push it on them, like you're selling cars or something."

I had a couple of beers, and with my confidence simmering, I returned to the front entrance and met a couple of the young folk who talked there before going inside.

"Before I leave,' I said, "I just have to let you know that I have the best dope in town. All you have to do is sniff the stuff, and believe me, you'll have a great time."

The college kids didn't know what to say, but it was obvious that there was a leader of the bunch, and I tried to appeal to his need to make his party last all night long. They wanted to see the small baggie of dope that I had. The leader looked at it and said, "I'll try some. How much does it cost?"

"Only twenty dollars for the bag. What do you say?"
Just like a leader, the young kid handled it like a pro. He
simply fished out a twenty, and I gave him the bag. I also
gave him a small slip of paper with my number on it.

"After you try it, let me know. I have the best dope in
town. Let me know if you'd like any more. It's just a little
harmless fun is all."

The bar tender saw what I was doing, and when I drifted
back to Gypsy, he said, "you guys better be careful around
here. There's a lot of competition in this city. This whole
area already has its dope fiends. For a little taste of what you
got, I can show you more people who may want what you
got."

"How much are we greasing you with?" asked Gypsy.

"How does five a bag sound?"

"We'll think about it," said Gypsy, the mastermind of
all of our plans.

We stayed there outside for a little while, but when we
saw that business was turning fairly flat at this experimental
bar that she found, we both went back home to the 'hood, and
she stayed with me for the night. I couldn't have been
happier while in bed with her, nudging close to her body in
an attempt to feel comfortable within this unknown world
that she had thrust me into.

I awoke the next afternoon. Gypsy was gone. I had little idea where or when she left or why. Somehow, she had untangled herself from my body and returned to her mother's place in Rensselaer earlier that morning. I guess I must have been tired, because she left a note. It said, 'try the colleges.' And I hated the idea of selling to college and university kids, but at that time, I didn't have a choice. We were still hurting for money, and a couple of bags to any of these kids meant that I could easily re-up with the main dealer from whom we bought the original heroin. It would give the main dealer more confidence in us if we sold out in the first couple of days

Later on that morning, after a more bountiful sleep, I knew that slinging bags of dope in the area colleges would have caused big problems. Their security plan had guards at every class building along with security cameras darting this way and that, both outside the buildings and within them. I took one look at the first campus I visited. Security guards were posted near the student center where most students ate their lunch and talked about their classes. I immediately thought it a better idea to position myself closer to the main city, farther away from the campuses, and wait for sales at the bus stops these university and college kids used every day and at all hours. I looked at each kid at the bus stops I visited, but none of them seemed to be heroin types. I had to wait around for those with ear and nose piercings, colorful tattoos, and black leather clothing to come around, which they did, especially that afternoon.

I saw a young woman coming towards the bus stop. I was damn nervous, as anyone would be at that time, because the young girl had that heroin-chic style to her that the young people had in larger cities further south and west of Albany.

"You want smoke?" I tried.

"You mean weed?" she asked.

"Something a little stronger than that."

"Hash?"

"No, but you're getting warmer. How about some H?"

"Heroin?"

"Yeah. Have you ever tried the stuff?"

"Yeah," she said. "How much are you selling?"

"For you, how does twenty a bag. It's really good dope. Came up all the way across from Middle East."

"Okay," said the girl, handing over a twenty-dollar bill.

Charlie quickly put the bag of heroin in her palm. The bus came, and she was off. I moved around to a number of different bus stops and found similar good fortune. By midafternoon, I had sold the whole half-bundle. Gypsy would take her cut of the money, and I went straight to the dealer's house and re-upped. This time, he gave me a full-bundle, which was ten bags of heroin to sell, the wholesale value being one-hundred and twenty dollars.

The man also showed his happiness by giving me a few additional bags of the brown dope to sell to whomever I wanted. He made it clear that I must now come to him for all of my dope needs and not to anyone else. There was way too much competition over the drug to the point that people were killing each other in the streets and these open air market places on every corner in this section of Albany taken over by thugs who pushed only their own brand of it. If I happened to step on their toes by selling the junk to the wrong person, I could easily be killed.

I had to be careful. So far, though, hanging around the bus stops seemed to work. I guess even the young people in the area trusted a beaming white New England face selling them heroin. The color of my skin made me trustworthy around these kids who hopped on and off the buses, kids who were intellectual fighters and wanted to edify their rebellious sides by trying the stuff. They learned how to trust me. I gave them my home number, and they took the liberty of calling me whenever they needed a bag or a bundle or even more. The money soon followed.

I paid Gypsy and the man we went to for the re-up. I kept the rest. So just to break it down, I had already sold a half-bundle, netting me one-hundred dollars. From that, I put fifty aside for Gypsy, and with the remaining money, I bought a ten-bag bundle from the main dealer. Everyone was happy at this rudimentary stage - the white college kids, myself, Gypsy, and the dope dealer, who admitted that he went down to the Bronx to get the stuff. Things worked out well. And I wanted Gypsy to marry me, now that the cash kept rolling in, now that I had returned to the white side of the fence and continued to make the kids happy, now that I was spending more time with the white culture in Albany instead of the isolated black side of town.

After a couple of weeks of meeting kids at the bus stops on their way to college, I was making too much money to keep in my own pocket. I opened up a bank account and made timely deposits almost every afternoon downtown near Empire State Plaza. No one at the bank really cared, even though a couple of them did have questions. A few of them eyed me a little, but again, they did their jobs and hoped the day would end as soon as they had arrived that morning. I just told them that I was an international global businessperson. As long as the cash rolled in, I could dress up as Ronald McDonald or Bozo the Clown, and they still wouldn't care.

Gypsy and I sensed, though, that something wasn't right. Maybe we were moving closer to each other? We had hit success too early, and something was bound to go wrong.

After one night of selling at the bus stops, I found Gypsy walking on the main avenue on her way to an appointment, at least that's what she said, and I immediately took her home with me. We both had the luxury of time and growing wealth. She came to my apartment, undressed, sat on my bed, and smoked crack.

"Why can't we get married, Gypsy? We have enough money. We've known each other for a while now. We like each other, right?"

"I like you, Charlie, yes."

She finished her hit, put the glass pipe on the floor, and rolled into me.

"I can't marry you, Charlie."

"Why not? I can take care of you. We're rising up the food chain. What's so wrong with marriage?"

"You seem to forget. I am a hooker, and you're still my client."

"I don't care about that."

"Well, you should. I do not want to get married."

"But you're not telling me why. You don't need to be a sex worker anymore. You're with me. We'll have plenty of money soon. All I have to do is sell to the students uptown. I just don't understand you."

"The more you don't understand about me, the better."

"Why's that? You don't ever want to be understood? That would drive any person crazy."

"I am crazy."

"I've noticed," I said.

She kissed my lips and then pulled the covers over her. She was tired, and I was tired of arguing with her. Once again, I found myself falling asleep within the bliss and warm comfort of Gypsy's body next to mine. She was soft and warm, just like I wanted her to be. The marriage question still perplexed me, but there was nothing I could do about it. She must have had her own troubles. Yet she was making money too, off of the cut I promised her.

We laid low, though. We weren't about to buy gold or silver, go on an extended vacation, or get a new sports car. We played the roles of the humble and the oppressed couple in the harsh neighborhood. Anything else would have gotten us into trouble, not only by the police and the few years in jail that would follow, but also the rival gangs who must have heard about our early successes. We had to lay low.

Somehow, these rival gangs in the 'hood had the developed intuition of finding people who made money and hurting their progress by taking their business away. They weren't mistaken. Gypsy and I pulled in a lot of money from the white side of the city without anyone knowing about it except our clients and the man who wholesaled the dope. We were both comfortable laying low. We did things like go out for dinner at the nearest mall. We went clothes shopping for both myself and her. I even called Cash up and asked if he could have used a few dollars.

"What about you?" asked Cash.

"I don't need any money. I have plenty here."

"Where's here?"

"Same place. Gypsy and I moved in together."

"Alright, Charlie, tell me the truth. What kind of trouble have you two gotten into? Both of you together probably can't even make a thin dime."

"We've struck it rich, let's just put it that way."

"You're headed for trouble if you hang around Gypsy too much. I've already told you this."

"Anyway, I just wanted to call to see if you needed anything."

"How did you come across so much money in such little time?"

"Gypsy has a connection."

"A connection to who?"

"You're not going to like this."

"I don't like it already, and you haven't even told me what you guys are into yet."

"We deal."

After a long and thorough silence, Cash said, *"You realize that what you're doing can get you killed, right? It's either that, or you'll go to jail for twenty years. You realize that, don't you?"*

"Yes, Cash, but..."

"Don't bother me about it. I don't want to hear about it. And don't call me from jail when you're caught. The next time I speak to you is when you get a normal job with normal people in a normal place."

"I don't think you realize how much money we're making here."

"The money won't last. That's all I want to say to you."

"But Cash, I - "

He hung up the phone after that. The conversation with him had disappointed me. If anyone, I thought Cash would be the most understanding of all, but he wasn't. I don't know if he were either jealous or insulted that he worked full days at the junkyard for next to nothing or not, but suddenly I was a big player in the wealthiest parts of the city making boatloads of cash. Either way, I didn't want to stop making money. Gypsy felt the same way when I brought it up with her.

"So, when do we stop, Gypsy? "When do we say enough is enough?"

She rolled over in bed to light up a cigarette. She sucked in hard and said, "never."

"Never?"

"Was I not clear? Never."

"I think we have enough right now to bow out, take the money, and run as fast as we can. I'm concerned that no one is going to let us leave Albany with this money we've been saving at the bank. Even the bank is getting suspicious."

"You worry too much."

"And you aren't worried at all?"

"We have a lot more to go. We need to collect the money and deal with our clients quietly. No one knows who you are. You're just one more white man in a sea of other whites. The pigs usually target the black neighborhoods. They don't police the white areas. We can make a lot, and then we'll get out. We'll disappear to the islands or even to South America."

"I sure hope you know what you're doing."

"If we wait a few weeks and do what we're doing, we'll have enough cash to last us a lifetime. Imagine that? I wouldn't have to take to the streets, and you wouldn't have to work minimum wage jobs. We'll be relieved of all of this New York pressure."

"How many more days?"

"Let's give it a month. Are you ready to re-up again?"

"Yeah, I am."

The man who dealt it to us wholesale was impressed by our productivity. He attributed it to working the white neighborhoods and my looking like a nerdish, scholarly fellow, which is what people thought of me already. Our wholesale man had confidence in us. And once the orders from the clients came in, we moved up to buying bricks of heroin which we would purify, and cut. We'd then call over our clients to my apartment to purchase. At one point, we had five or six visitors per day, and we had collected about five-hundred dollars a day. I wanted to have fun at the casino the next town over, but Gypsy insisted that we keep it quiet and not make too much noise from our newfound fortune. She said that she wanted enough money so that we could afford a team of good lawyers, in case we got caught.

Reluctantly, I went along with this request, even though my heart beat fully with the pent-up demand for nice dinners, vacations, and moving into an apartment that was much bigger than where I lived. In fact, I wanted out of my own apartment pretty badly.

Gypsy, however, declared the need to move as some kind of sexual energy that needed release. Every time I wanted to move, we made love, and while on top of me, she reassured me that my apartment was fine. All I needed was stress relief. The way she went about it worked. I made love to her at least once a day, and soon, I forgot about getting new things in favor of the attention she gave me. She spent all my money, sure, but I couldn't have been happier with our arrangement.

It wasn't until she disappeared for a little while that I got nervous. I called her a few times, but she didn't respond. I looked for her out on the street but couldn't find her. I even went to our wholesale dealer and asked if she were available to talk to, but she wasn't there. We had all of this cash, and I was unsure if I should continue dealing without her or stop until I found her again. Since I had a brick of dope to move, I decided that it was still worth the risk even without her.

On the nights that I did visit the bus stops surrounding the university, I could feel the youth soaking my bones. I grew envious of them, now that I was embarking upon an uneasy adulthood. While dealing the stuff, there was something that I missed. I wanted what they had - the freedom to thrive, and the freedom to drink or smoke whenever they felt like it. I saw my own youth in them, as it fluttered away into the real adult need for making money. I figured that the rest of the world was like this. Just acquire money at all costs, and for some reason the world opened up - all of those beautiful women, the alcohol, the music, and the ability to travel anywhere. This is what I wanted. The youth, however, could break the law and get away with it, just because they were both young and foolish at their age, and their ages had been institutionalized in law and order. They get the wonderful first slap on the wrist, and the scare them with a night in jail, and maybe from that they stay out of jail.

Meanwhile, I'm watching out for cops and selling the five bundles of the brick bag-by-bag. Even people whom I had never seen before wanted the dope that I dealt. When I saw this happening, I knew already that we must have been watched by the police. Yet since I was a white boy in a sea of other whites clamoring for me at the bus stops, I just went on with what I was doing, and the cops didn't find me, nor did they care to find me. They would know only if I were a black man at a bus stop with other whites buying my stuff.

It took just one night for me to sell the whole brick of heroin. But I still needed to see Gypsy, because she didn't show up later that night. Nevertheless, I went to our dealer man's place and re-upped. I bought a sleeve of dope this time, and the dealer thought that I was some wizard of the bus stops. Even he worried about anyone nearby pinching us for some money. We still had to lay low, but all of those damned college students wanted more and more of it. We were getting too big for own good.

"Where's Gypsy?" I asked the wholesaler at his door.

"I don't know," he said.

"I think she's missing. Something must have gone wrong."

"Take it easy, Charlie, would ya? She probably went to Rensselaer to visit her mother. She'll turn up someplace. Why don't you come in?"

The wholesaler sat me down on his futon and went to the fridge to get a couple bottles of beers for us. The bottles were ice cold and went down smoothly without the usual shots of liquor that may have taken their place.

"She's gone," I said. "What if she doesn't want to come back?"

The wholesaler took a long swig of his beer and said, "listen, you need to re-up. How about a sleeve? That's ten bundles at eight-hundred dollars."

That was way too much dope to peddling out on the street. I didn't want to get nabbed.

"I'll take it," I said, "but it may take some time to re-up. What if the police come to get me?"

"Believe me," said the wholesaler. "The police don't care unless someone's shot. Take this sleeve. I also want to show you something."

He vanished into his bedroom for a moment and brought out a gigantic gold chain that one would wear around a thick, black neck.

"I've been saving this for you," said the wholesaler. "This is yours. This is the most I've ever earned before, a black man who lives in the hood, but sells his dope to white America. We need more people like you, Charlie. This chain, I bought for you. It is my gift and a token of my appreciation."

"Wow. This is heavy. How could you afford such a thing? It's beautiful. It must have cost you a fortune." "Nah," said the wholesaler.

And just then the doorbell rang. The wholesaler permitted two women to enter. They showed up at the front door with their skimpy clothing and white smiles. Yes, to Charlie astonishment, the two women were white and dressed for nighttime extravagances.

"Charlie, I went you to meet Bella and Diane." "Hello," I said, shaking their hands.

"God, you really are a nerd," laughed the wholesaler. "Why don't you stop shaking the women's hands and kiss them on the cheek as a greeting instead?"

After I did that, the two women burst out into happiness. I could tell that they had, at one time, been formal and hung out with the players of the night, but now they had let down their guard, grabbed my arms, and walked with me to the limo waiting for us downstairs.

"Wait, don't you want to even know my name?"

198

One of the women kissed me on the cheek. The other, kissed me on the lips. Apparently, it was party time, and the last thing on my mind was Gypsy.

The driver drove us twenty minutes into Schenectady, while both Bella and Diane did lines on each other's necklines. Then they unbuttoned my shirt and did lines on my chest. We also drank from a bottle of campaign. By the time we arrived, the driver pulled into the new casino in Schenectady.

It was a place I tried to stay away from when I worked at the junkyard, but now, there was so much money and so much decadence enshrined within the heavy gold chain draped over my neck, that I suddenly had too much money to keep storing in the bank. The night was wide open with two sexy women wearing hardly anything at all, their arms slipped through mine, pulling me along a red carpet to the casino's entrance door.

I almost wept with joy as these two women surrounded me and then escorted me inside. The bouncers nodded us through, as though I were someone of importance. I didn't mistake this extra special treatment in a party-place that would normally have kept me out just several months ago. I looked like an eighteen-year-old with seasoned professionals on either side of me, bundled up close to me from the nighttime breeze.

Both Bella and Diane knew how nervous I had become, as nearly everyone there looked at us. I was even afraid that people lining the bars along the way to the casino floor may have thought that I had paid for all of this, this kind of dream vacation or break from the everyday, which was easily found in Albany but in no way found in Schenectady. Maybe I needed to have fun for a change instead of remaining so adamantly business-oriented and focused so much on Gypsy, whom I worked hard to forget that night. I still wanted to marry her.

While the two women were fun and ebullient in their demeanor, I hung on to them tight, hoping not to look like a kid but more of an adult who knew what he was doing. I shook under the spotlight. Even the dealers had to admit that these two women and I stole the show. Their table games were ready for me, and I laid down a hundred-dollar bill at an empty blackjack table. It took only one hand like this to lose a hundred bucks. It took less than a minute, but I didn't care. Back in the world of the junkyard, such a loss would have been unforgivable. But now, though, the hundred-dollar loss hardly mattered. We three laughed at the loss, since I had more money than I knew what to do with.

I wanted a beer, and the three of us, laughing into the oxygenated space of the casino air, drifted to the sidelines where a crowded club sent me into waves of optimism that I had abandoned a long time ago.

From the pulsing lights, the people dancing hard to the beats of the dee-jay, and the plumes of smoke from dry ice that fogged every corner of the room, everyone seemed to love it, even though I had little idea why they loved it. And then I figured it out. Both Bella and Diane said that they needed to powder their noses, but before leaving me on the dance floor, they gave me a small yellow pill to take. They left so quickly for the ladies' room that I didn't even have the chance to ask what kind of pill it was.

I took the mighty yellow pill before I had finished my first beer. After that beer, I didn't feel like drinking any more of the stuff. For some reason, I felt a little bloated while looking at the dancing and the women from my watchtower of the bar. I also canvased the dance floor for Bella and Diane. I also wondered when the pill, whatever it was, would take effect.

When the women returned to the bar a little later in the evening, they were very high, probably still on cocaine. I had fallen in love with humanity when they arrived. An eternal love. I was no saint any more. My prolonged innocence fell away from me like a knight's strong armor, giving me the freedom to do whatever it was I wanted to do out in Schenectady with these two women.

Exactly when the women came back, I couldn't say, but when they returned, they dragged me onto the dance floor, and I could do little more but slide along with them and their firm, warm bodies. They twerked whenever they saw fit. I was on fire for these women, and instead of heading home, the women had reserved the Presidential suite for us, which was located on the penthouse of the hotel.

By the time the party heated up, these women wanted to take me up to the room, and I let them. I can't remember anything more about the evening, other than the postcard left on the hotel's dresser said that they 'had a great time, and let's do it again.' They also kissed the postcard, exposing a perfect trace of their lips in red lipstick. Meanwhile the cleaning people continued to knock on the door, wondering when I'd vacate the room, now that it was two hours after check out. I found myself naked under thin sheets and incredibly hungover. We're talking fierce nausea and an upset stomach so bad that I didn't want to leave the hotel room at all. I was more than willing for another expensive night at the hotel instead.

I donned my clothes and made it down to the lobby. There was no limo there waiting for me this time, though. I took the express bus back to Albany. I wanted to talk to our wholesaler that afternoon. I wanted to know what he meant by such a gesture. I was terribly confused by this turn of events, especially since I could hardly remember staying in any casino at all. When I knocked on his door, he seemed pleased to let me in.

"So, how was it?" he asked.

"I hardly remember anything."

"That means that it must have been a great night."

"I can only recall sitting at the blackjack table and losing all my money with the two women sitting next to me. We were all having a good time. They even left me a note before they bolted from the place."

"Sounds like you had a great time."

"Well, now I have to re-up, because my clients must be jonesing for more."

"Y'know something," said the wholesaler. "You're my good luck charm."

"Who? Me?"

"Yeah. You've re-upped more than any other dealer I have. I'm lucky enough to be your plug. You must have a lot of clients by now. You've steadily bought more than anyone else. You're the best move I've ever made." "Well, I just wanted to stop by, because I'm feeling very sick, and I wanted to know if you heard anything about what I did last night."

"I have no idea. But everything is okay. Everything is safe. Everything will fall into place after you get over your hangover. You must be feeling pretty sick right now."

"I'm just so damn nauseous. It's a terrible feeling."

"Listen, just go home, sleep it off, take a shower, change your clothes, and come back later."

"Also, I'm missing Gypsy."

"Gypsy? I haven't heard from her. When did you see her last?"

"It's been a few days. She vanished, and now I have no idea where she went."

"Hell, I don't know anything. I can ask around, though."

"You'd do that for me?"

"Yeah, no sweat. God, you really like Gypsy."

"I think I'm in love with her."

"Shit. That's not the way to go. Maybe she left, because she saw it unfolding. All of that lovey-dovey bullshit. If I hear from her, I'll let you know."

"Let me get some shit done, and I'll return tonight to reup, okay? I'd rather be carrying at night."

"You're my good-luck charm. Don't forget it. And I'm your plug. Don't forget about that either."

The bus ride home was torture, even though it was a brilliant, golden day sponsored by the sunshine that watched us our bus high from its perch in the afternoon sky. Finally, a rough spring had turned into a relaxing summer, and even though I was sick from the night at the casino, I couldn't stop thinking of Gypsy.

I called her several times, and got her answering machine. Missing her was both crude and visceral, but at least my nausea subsided while lying in my messy bed in my messy apartment starting to feel hungry for an egg and cheese sandwich from the Arab convenience store down the block. But I was still too tired. I fell asleep involuntarily.

I awoke when the buzzer to my apartment went off with scream. I raced to the lobby in a pair of boxers and a tee shirt. Gypsy stood there behind the glass door. She didn't look well at all. Her face seemed pockmarked from old acne and a lack of makeup, and her hair stood on end in all directions. She looked terrible, her clothes dirty, her purse penniless as usual, and I wanted to know why. I let her in, and we went straight to the second floor of my piece of shit apartment.

As soon as she entered, she knew the place had to be cleaned. She suddenly found a reason for tidying up. She looked so drugged out, that I had to get her some crack to keep her from going to detox. Actually, the hospital would have helped immensely.

I called my plug and told him that I found Gypsy. I asked him for a few rocks of good quality crack. God bless him, because he sent over a runner right away, and when Gypsy fell out of her sickness and into a more comfortable space because of the crack, she kissed me on the lips and immediately took one of her long vacations in the bathroom, added by a long shower. Gypsy had been cursed by her drug habits, and a hospital would have worked in the present situation. I started to hate the crack that she smoked. She refused a hospital. She wanted more crack.

I requested that she go to the hospital. It looked like she had been playing in the gutters of Albany again. For once, I did not bother her in the bathroom. As far as I was concerned, she could stay there for a whole week without a word from me, now that she had the capacity to hide from others or get into trouble on her own when she stayed away from me. After her shower, she slept on my bed for a few hours. I figured she was tired from whatever she was out there doing. Maybe her adventures gave her a reason to marry me, because no one could take care of her like I could. I realized this as soon as she fell asleep. I was the one whom God chose to care for her. She was a wreck of a person, and only if she agreed to be my wife could I turn her life in a positive direction as well as my own life, which somehow seemed so vacant now, even with the money I had earned selling dope and the wild night at the casino. On the bed she rolled over into me. She was barely awake but awake enough to answer my question, "would you marry me,

Gypsy?"

"Let's not talk about that," she mumbled.

"When are we going to talk about it, then?"

"In a little while, okay?"

"No. I want to talk about it now."

She sat up in bed, still sleepy from wherever she went and took a long drag from her crack pipe and then a menthol cigarette to round off the hit.

"I'm not that kind of person," she said, finally.

"You've never been married. How would you know?"

"How many times have I told you, Charlie. I'm a hooker. I make money that way. I have plenty of people looking after me.

I'm not the marrying type. I don't want to get married."

"But I'm making money hand over fist. I'm making about five-hundred dollars a day."

"I don't care."

"But I can take care of you. You don't have to walk the streets anymore."

"I love you to death, Charlie, but I'm not marrying anyone."

"How about being my girlfriend? See me exclusively. What if that's all that I ask of you?"

"I need some more sleep, Charlie. Let's talk about this later."

A hot and humid day gave way to a few rain showers, and when I awoke after a long, hungover nap, Gypsy had left. She was no longer next to me. I even called her name throughout the cave I had been living in. No answer. She was gone again.

I tried to get through the day as best as I could. I visited my clients at various bus stops along the way to the university. I also wanted Cash to get into the game with me. I was making so much money that I didn't know what to do with all of it. I kept on delivering large deposits to the local bank, and as long as I paid them a premium to launder the money, they didn't raise any flags to anyone. They kept on accepting the large deposits week after week. But I felt like I owed it to Cash, to convince him that what I did was a foolproof plan of making it rich. It hurt me to know that he still labored at the junkyard. I wanted him by my side. I wanted to make him rich, so that he could afford, not only a flight to Fiji, but a whole damn mansion there. I called him after the day was done, when things ran smoothly without any deviant adventures.

"What's up, Charlie! Long time, no speak. How's life in the fast lane?"

"Makin' a lot of money, Cash."

"So I guess that makes you a gangster, eh?"

"Not yet, but things are heading in that direction."

"Great. Money was what you were after, and now you have it. What are you planning on doing with it?"

"I don't know yet, but I want to help you with that trip to Fiji you were talking about."

"Oh, you mean the dream that was Fiji? Just don't have the cash right now. Why? What's up?"

"If you work for me, you'd be able to have a mansion in both Fiji and Albany. What do you think of that?"

"You mean I'll be able to find a house in jail or Death Row?"

"Aren't you tired of the junkyard? You're hardly making a living, and I know you're on the government tit. That's no secret."

"I am starting to get tired of the junkyard, and I do get a little help from the government. But I don't want to end up jail. I can't handle jail, Charlie. I don't want to look over my back for the rest of my life."

"This is nothing to worry about. Work for me for one week is all I'm asking. You'll be richer than you ever dreamed."

"I don't know. I'm happy, Charlie. I know I work hard and all, but my black ass in this white world is actually happy for a change."

"You'll never make it to Fiji."

"You might be right, but I don't want to get into any trouble."

"Just think about it, okay? With a week's work, you'll be amazed at how much you can make. I mean, don't try to hide it anymore. I know you're struggling, but I need someone like you. First and foremost, you're my best friend, and second, I can use someone who's honest and sincere with me."

"Let me think about it," he said. *"I'll let you know this weekend. We'll go out for dinner."*

"Sounds good to me. Where do you want to eat?"

"You pick the place."

I brimmed with confidence after talking with Cash. I wanted him to make as much money as possible, because in a small way, I had been lonely, and I wanted a trusted friend to guide me. Whether or not he would work was what really mattered, and if I convinced him, maybe he would do it. I wanted to expand my clients to include people of color. I knew it might have been dangerous, because I may have been stepping on gang territory, but I knew that I could do it with my plug's help. I went to go see my plug to pick up more supplies and start my day in and around the college crowd.

"So, you're doing a little too well, eh?" he said when he opened the door."

I walked in and sat on his couch.

"Has anyone taken notice of you?"

"Not yet. I look like a college student, so no one has found me."

"Good. What brings you here, then?"

"I want a couple of sleeves."

"My God, a couple? You're selling out fast, aren't you?"

"Yeah."

"Hey, but you need to stay low."

"I'm inviting a friend to come on board."

"Okay. You'll be his plug, I take it?"

"Yeah," I said, "but something tells me that I'm in danger. I don't want anyone knowing what I'm doing, especially in gangland."

"You're trying to corner the whole market. You're right. Word is bound to get out that you're the most successful dealer in this small-ass town."

My wholesaler said he'd be right back. He disappeared into his bedroom for a minute and returned with a cold Glock automatic in his hand.

"Here. Take this," he said.

This cold, desperate instrument fit flatly in my palm.

"It's loaded. Keep the thing with you, and we'll have no problems."

"I've never held a gun before."

"Well, get used to it. Summer is almost here, and things will get dangerous in the 'hood. Also, in these white areas. You'll see a bunch of other niggas trying to do what you are doing. Make sure they stay away from your clientele."

I tried putting the gun in my front pocket, but my plug instructed me to tuck the gun in the slip of my back. He gave me a couple of sleeves after I had forked over two-grand for it. That was still the going rate. He also gave me a box of ammo to load the gun. After shaking his hand, I left his place and returned to my own, empty apartment. The plan was not to move from the apartment just yet. I could have easily afforded a big house in the suburbs, but I wanted Gypsy to live with me, at least as my exclusive girlfriend.
Who knew if that would happen?

I called Cash that night. I definitely needed to know if he would help me move the sleeves of heroin to the many more clients that waited for it elsewhere. I had about twenty messages on my voicemail from clients who were dying for my stuff. But first, I wanted to know what Cash had decided.

"Okay, Charlie, you got me," he said when I called.

"You mean, you'll do it?"

"Yeah. I could use the money. You were right."

"Money talks, bullshit walks."

I met Cash that night at the mall. I wanted to take him to a nice place, maybe the Chocolate Factory or something similar. We ended up going to Delmonico's along Central Avenue. I wanted meat, and Cash, who had grown gaunt and fatigued from the torture of hauling away metal, needed the protein as well. He was so hungry that he ate a big-ass steak in record time.

"God, Cash. What happened to you?"

"I've been working hard lately," he said. "I can't pretend that I can afford to live here anymore."

"I got you covered, Cash. You won't have to feel this way ever again. The job is so easy. Just avoid these police cars. Just avoid the rising number of gang-associated fatalities."

"Great," he smiled. "Is that all?"

"I want you to sell in black communities, but wealthier black communities. Not where I live, in other words. You have to move upscale. If you sell in the 'hood you're bound to attract the other gangs that are already selling to poor addicts. We don't want that.

I want you to find upscale black neighborhoods and sell it there. Get to know people, especially young blacks. They think they can do anything. It's good you have a car too. Mine is on its way."

"What'd you get?"

"A Jaguar."

"Nice!"

"You'll be able to afford one too, if you do well, and I can tell you that it is not that hard."

"Maybe for you," said Cash, "but for me?"

"I do see your point, Cash. It is dangerous, but only in these poor communities. A lot of people there sell to get by, and they have little connection to the working world. You would be at the high end. You won't have to sell in the South End or Arbor Hill. Leave those sections to the idiot gangs. You need to go to the apartment buildings in the student ghetto. Your future clients are mixed in with the young, so you'll be okay. Just do it quietly, and sell to the few people that you trust. I'm starting you out with a half bundle, which is basically five bags of quality shit that my plug gets and then passes to me. Take your time selling it. There's no rush, and it takes time to develop a clientele anyway. I know you need the money, but please, do not rush. Be patient. Use street knowledge at all times."

"Street knowledge, huh?"

"You got it."

"Hey, I studied in school!"

"I know you did, Cash, but who else can offer you more money than you've seen working all of those jobs you've had combined? No more struggle, Cash. And no one will fuck with you."

I carefully showed him the gun that my plug gave me. It sat snuggly in the small of my back, but for some reason, I knew that I didn't need it as much as Cash did. I gave him the gun that my plug had given me.

"Are you serious?"

"Shhh. Lower your voice a little. I'm sliding it under the table. You may need this."

"Jesus, Charlie, I don't know. I mean, I know these steaks cost money, and maybe a man like myself can't make enough on his own honest fate, but Jeez, Charlie, an automatic weapon? I've never dealt with a gun before."

"Learn how to use it before you sell those five bags, okay?"

"Hey, you got it. I'll start tomorrow." I also slid him two hundred in cash.

"Have a good night tonight. Go to the

215

casino with a girl or a friend of yours.

You can even ask your friends if they

want to become dealers."

"I don't think I'm there yet," he said gravely, as though someone in the restaurant died right in front of us.

"Just aim and shoot. Go to a shooting range if you have to. I think with the whites, there's not that much danger - maybe by the cops, but that's about it. If you're selling to upper class blacks, you shouldn't get into any trouble at all, but the gun is your insurance policy. If someone aims at you, you aim at them and pull the trigger. And then run back to Arbor Hill and hide."

"I get it, Charlie."

"You should start making five-hundred a day if you want it."

"Yeah. I could use that."

"I'm going to live my dream of living with Gypsy in the suburbs, and after you learn a thing or two, you'll be on your way to Fiji with all this money to marry someone from there."

"I can use it. I think my back is giving out."

"That's what minimum wage will get you. Don't be fooled by all these shitty jobs. We both know that we can't live off of those jobs."

The steak that we ate was probably the best steak I had ever tasted. It went down nicely with a tall glass of ice-cold beer, the meat of the steak buttery smooth and tender with perfect marbling. We stayed for quite a while that night. We both got drunk and hit on the ladies until the manager of the place asked us to leave. It's funny, because the bars in Albany wouldn't let anyone get drunk anymore. The slightest aberration in behavior, and they throw you out to the curb.

We left finally, and for a couple of weeks things had moved ahead. Cash deposited his money in the same bank I used. I had him meet the banker in charge of my account. Cash had no problem just sliding on through, as he gave the banker some money under the table so that the bulk of his money could be laundered just like mine.

As far as our relationship went, he really became my best friend. My plug and I also had a friendship, but it was always business with him. He had all the money the world would allow. We needed dealers, and Cash was all mine. I'd re-up him just like my plug re-upped me. Green money could have been falling from the trees that summer, and we just raked up the green garbage, these leaves of cash, and did it over and over again.

We didn't know where to store the money, but my plug took care of it. We used a combination of small, independent banks to cover everything up. We went to the casinos just to have a good time of it. We ate gourmet meals. We even started to buy real estate in the area. We had everything we could ever ask for. It was terrible, though, when Cash called in from a jail phone trying desperately to reach me. It had been a month since he started, and damn it, he got caught. I asked him over the jailhouse phone what the hell happened.

"Just calm down, Cash, and tell me everything."

"I was doing my apartment-building deal, when one of my clients tried to rob me of my money and my sleeve. I shot him in the leg, which stopped him, but someone at the building called it in. I did like you said. I ran as fast as I could, until the cops beat me in a foot race going back to Arbor Hill. Shit, man. I think I'm in a lot of trouble."

"Just hold on, Cash, okay. What was your bail set for?"

"Because I carried a weapon, the judge denied bail."

"Shit, Cash. Listen, I'll get the best lawyers in Albany to fight for your release. Don't worry."

"My life is over, Charlie. I'm stuck here for a long time."

"Just be patient."

"Some people are messing with me here. I think they want to knife. They know I've been dealing where they can't."

"Just hold on and pray a lot. I'm sending in the best Goddamned lawyers this city has ever seen. Just stay calm, do everything the guards ask you to do for now. I'm going to get you out. You have my word."

"Hurry, if you can. I don't think I can handle it in here."

"Just hang on, buddy, okay? We're gonna get you out of here."

"I guess I'll never make it to Fiji, eh?"

"You will make it to Fiji, damnit. I promise you that. Just think of all of those South Asian women, those warm beaches, that big mansion you'll be living in, those kids you'll have. You'll make it there, God-damn you, Cash. I promise you that."

Interestingly enough, I felt the same worry he felt. Although I had never been pinched by the police before, I understood why the police would be searching around for drugs in the upscale black neighborhoods of Albany, as though these neighborhoods were experimental bio-domes which many hoped would remain livable for many years to come.

I called my plug, and he gave me a list of several lawyers who were the best in the area when dealing with cases such as Cash's. He had been caught dealing, and he carried an unlicensed armed fire weapon. From what Cash told me, they caught him with the heroin in his pocket and the gun tucked into the waist of his denim jeans.

As soon as I confirmed everything with the lawyer, I took my new Jaguar down to the county jail where he was being held. A thick plexiglass barrier separated us, and we talked through a bulky yellow hand receiver. He looked like shit. He was rich now, but he looked like shit.

"Jesus, Cash. What the hell happened to you in here? It seems you're a little, well, a little unkempt."

"I can't eat the food in here," he said. "I haven't eaten anything since I've been in here. There's no bail, so I can't leave this shithole. I'm starting to lose it, Charlie. I just had to shoot the sonofabitch who tried to rob me."

"What are you losing exactly?"

"Losing my mind, Charlie. I'm starting to lose my mind in here."

"Now just calm down, okay, Cash? You can do the time until the sentencing, okay? My guess is that you'll do some jail time, but this is your first offense, so you are bound to stay only a short time until they release you. Remember, I have the best lawyers in the Capital District who are working hard on your case, and I can easily pay for all of them."

"Don't do that to yourself, Charlie. At least let me pay for it."

"I got you into this, and I'm gonna get you out. Just sit tight, do your time nicely, and I'll be visiting you often. How does that sound?"

"Terrible."

"I know, my brother, I know, but we're going to get you out. You have my word on it. And when you do come out, all of that money will be waiting for you, along with an extra eight percent interest. I'm keeping it all safe."

"Charlie, I don't think I can handle it in here. I can't eat, it's so noisy that I can't sleep, my bed is a metal tray, and the boredom is driving me straight down into my own personal hell."

"Just wait it out, okay? We'll do what we can do."

When we hung up our receivers, Cash, in his stiff orange jailhouse uniform, put his hand on the window and said, "please don't forget about me in here, Charlie, okay?"

"Nothing to worry about," I mouthed back to him.

After the lawyers went through the courts, I was told that Cash would have to spend about five years in jail, and then he'd be eligible for parole. The judge was too heavy on the side of law and order to have had my team of lawyers make any headway with his imperial decision. He came down hard, as there was a now serious heroin epidemic in the city.

By nailing Cash to the wall, he thought that he had made a difference. And meanwhile, I continued to sell dope without too much trouble. Also, there was something so privileged about being a white man that I never noticed before. Somehow, because I was white, society seemed to know more about what good I've brought to the world than the ugly bad things that I had been doing to others by selling them dope.

White people beg for understanding, and the media only reinforces this attempt to understand the good sides of whites. Meanwhile, blacks will always seem like gangsters, beggars, and thieves. They are the poor, living in drug infested shacks, always working on something illegal, always presenting their derelict side to audiences who are really very scared of them.

Where are those blacks who are cozy in the high-rises, the colleges, and the hospitals? They have made tons of money on hard work, have created such inventions that have startled and enlightened the American mind. You see, I needed to see this. I needed to know Cash, Gypsy, and my plug. I didn't want to follow the path of the racist, and so my mind had been cleansed by the dint of working in Albany and making connections, and finding a friend like Cash, and steadily doing way too well for my own good.

After a week of high sales, I knew I had to see Cash in the county jail. He would soon be transferred to state prison someplace upstate. My driver took me there on a rainy afternoon that I now remember so well.

When I went in the lobby to be escorted into the jail to see him, instead of taking me directly to the visitor's room, they brought me to a small office where an older black woman, who held authority over prison life, sat at a desk filled with papers and forms. She was the warden in uniform, and I was nervous as hell talking to her. I tried to find out if I had been found for wrong-doing.

"How are you related to Cassius Phillips?" she asked.

"You mean, Cash?"

"No. Cassius Phillips, which is his God-given name."

"I'm not related to him, as you can see."

"Believe me. I need to ask, and I've seen a lot. Just don't play stupid with me."

"I won't, ma'am," I said. "I am here to see him. I think I'm here for visiting hours. Right on schedule."

"But how do you know him?"

"We used to work at the junkyard. He's my best friend."

"Really? Who was his supplier?"

"Supplier of what?"

"You know what I'm talking about."

"I'm afraid I don't," I lied.

"So. you're just friends, eh?"

"That's what I'm telling you, ma'am. We used to work together, and I haven't seen him for a couple of weeks since my last visit. So, I thought I'd visit. "

Can you shut the door, please," she asked.

For some reason, I thought she'd lock me up for something that she knew I did, but she had me sit in front of her and even poured me a cup of dull, taxpayer's coffee.

"Son, I have a hard time telling this to people, so let me just be honest and frank with you. Cassius Phillips, your friend Cash, took his own life a couple of days ago. He hung himself in his jail cell by tying a towel to his toilet, thereby suffocating himself. I'm sorry to have to tell you this." "Are you sure?" I asked, incredulous.

"Yes, and I'm sorry. We're trying to locate his family. Do you have any idea where his family might be?"

"I don't. Cash was always a single guy. I didn't think he had any family."

"Someone has to collect the body."

"I just can't believe it. Him of all people? All he had to do was wait in here. I wanted to get him out, but I guess he couldn't handle it for one more miserable day in here."

"We see this a lot," said the warden. "He was an armed drug dealer, plain and simple. They find ways to make easy money. Well, it doesn't work out that way. Normally, it's these buyers that are white boys like yourself. But how you made a best friend with a junk collector is really beyond me. No one understands it, which is why I should arrest your white ass for being his supplier. But we both know that white boys get away with it, and the black community has to swallow another senseless death of a young black man."

"I see your point, but Cash really was my best friend. I just can't believe he would do something like that," as my eyes unlocked tears. "He was so good to me. You don't understand. No one understands me in this God-forsaken world. Why are we so apart by skin color? It just doesn't make sense. Cash never harmed anyone. You, warden or whoever you are, are too sad to see what beauty there is when men and women from different sides of the tracks help each other. You and your officers will never be able to see that."

"Maybe not. But this isn't a perfect world. It will never be. Never. Why do you think your friend is dead? I can tell that he was a good person and was selling drugs to make money, just like any other drug dealer locked up in this place.

"When I was a young kid growing up in an all-Black neighborhood, it was easy enough to see the killings, the shotgun rounds at night, the gangs huddling around convenience stories, the drugs that took people away, the jailhouses that are always stocked with hungry Black men. I didn't know how to end it either. But I can at least see with my own eyes that your friendship with him was real. But it couldn't last, just like all of this white and black together bullshit. Do you see what I'm telling you? You continue to sell your white drugs in black neighborhoods, and I, personally, will shoot you right in the skull. You understand that?"

"Yes, ma'am."

"For now, if you know of any family members that are actually related to him, you send them my way. Otherwise, I don't want to see your white face around here again. Understand?"

"Yes, ma'am."

"We'll contact you if you have to bury the body, okay?"

Turns out I did have to bury the body. Cash had few friends in the neighborhood, but no one knew of any family close to him. The few people at the funeral all agreed that he was a very hard worker, but never really had a chance once the cops imprisoned him.

I must have wept the whole time. I felt that my hands were too dirty to carry the casket and perform all these rituals to memorialize the dead. Most of us grieved right through, but for me the real grieving came when I had no one to call, no one on the street to talk to, no one to look after. His absence was indelibly sewn into my heart, almost as though someone had branded his heart into mine. I thought that I had enough money already, and maybe I should have quit while I was ahead. But after the brief, hurried funeral, after getting Cash a tombstone that was a tall, monumental fixture at any expensive or prestigious cemetery, I then reached out to Gypsy. I did not want the same thing to happen to her. So I called. She said she'd be over in an hour. It took her a full three.

As usual with her, I waited a long time for her arrival. She never did have a sense of good timing. She was always late and inert when she smoked her crack. I didn't know what to make of it. I realized then that it was not she who was the great challenge, but the crack cocaine that steadily brought her down. If she did it too much, she wouldn't have much of a brain left. When she arrived, I wanted to touch her, and after I kissed her lips, I told her that I wanted her to quit smoking all of that crack. She was a bad addict already. It was getting worse.

"Shut up, Charlie," she said.

"I'm being serious. That crack is holding you back from living a more fulfilling life. You need help in stopping. There's tons of help around here for that."

"Stop insulting my intelligence, Charlie. You think I don't know what I'm doing?"

"Did I say that? No."

She closed herself off in the bathroom for a while and did some strange yoga, hypnosis-shit that I never wanted to try with her. She stayed in there an hour before she came to bed. I couldn't understand her when she slid under my sheets. Her nude body, taut and smooth next to mine, had been the best feeling to it I've ever had with a woman. I tried not to dwell on wanting to marry her, even though I wanted to marry her. I didn't want to piss her off again and again.

I did tell her that Cash had died, and that maybe I should get out of the business, now that I had made all of that money that sat in the vaults of the banks we chose. I did want to stop. I had had enough.

"No more, huh?" she asked as she rested her head on my breast.

"I'm not into it," I said. "Look at what happened to Cash. I'm now carrying a gun wherever I go. This has gotten insane. It's insanity, and I want it to stop. I'm not happy dealing these drugs. One day I'm going to get pinched, I just know it."

"Shhh," she said. "Don't worry too much. Cash died, because he tried to land one of the most competitive markets in this city. You, on the other hand, are dealing to rich, white boys. Cash was caught, and that's what did him in. You're not responsible for his life."

"I think I am."

"It happens, Charlie, okay?"

She climbed on top of me. We made love as though our lives depended on it. For Gypsy, this may have been just another date, but for me, I wanted her so badly that even making love didn't suffice. Nevertheless, I didn't bring up marriage anymore. She hated when I did. I fell asleep with her in my arms, but she was gone by the next afternoon. I awoke with hot sunlight bathing my bed. I felt around for her, but she was gone, who knew where to.

I quickly donned my clothes and went to see my plug. I needed to return the gun and tell him that I had to quit, mainly due to what happened to Cash.

When I walked into his apartment, an immediate scent of marijuana hovered in the air. My plug had been smoking on a long, glass bong. He offered me some, but I refused.

"Cash had the harder run," he said. "There's so many competing gangs now. Not only is it easy getting pinched by the pigs, but they'll shoot anyone down who tampers with their business. I don't blame you that you want to quit. But I warn you, once you're in, it is very hard to get out. You must be fielding about twenty calls a day. Am I right?"

"Yeah," I said.

He took a long suck from his bong.

"Are you sure you don't want any? This is the best green we've had in Albany for some time."

"No. I'm alright."

"Do you want my honest opinion of you?"

"Go right ahead."

"I think you are really damn good at what you do. I'm your biggest supplier, and you have easily passed what it takes to be a dealer. Without a doubt, you are the best client I have."

"Thanks," I said.

"But you're naive. There's something very innocent about you, and on the street, that could either be good or bad. I know you're young, but in order to continue our business, you may have to use the gun I gave you."

"Hey, I don't want to hurt anyone."

"There's the naivety. Sometimes you have to hurt people to stay safe, to keep the business going. You must be making all types of money right now. You're also keeping your clients happy, which is important. Again, the time may come when someone steps on your toes, and you can't be nice about it. This is part of the deal, Charlie. And once you pull the trigger, the cycle of revenge starts over again. Someone will then be pointing the gun at you."

"I'm just selling to recreational clients right now. I stay away from the bad neighborhoods."

"Some of them will fall into addiction. Right now, there's a drug epidemic here in Albany, as I'm sure you know. The white people are flooding into our neighborhoods to buy. The pigs are rounding people up. This is a blessing and a curse, a blessing that we're gonna make tons more money, as the dope on the dealing on the street spirals out of control. And then there's the curse. We'll be sending a lot of addicts to their graves. It may be recreational right now, but eventually, you will have to hurt somebody. You may have to go to jail for killing a client. Does this make any sense to you? When you go further, you'll be dealing with this shit for the rest of your life. It never stops. My suggestion is that you quit while you're ahead. Or maybe you can lay low for a while, take a break, especially since your friend just died."

I thought my plug's advice seemed sound, and after meeting with him, I thought that I should take a break, as he advised. I did go to Cash's grave site again. He had distant relations who lived in Albany after all. They had placed a bouquet of flowers on the monument that I bought. I felt responsible for Cash's death. He may have been too ambitious in his attempt to deal, but I'm the one who had gotten him into the game. It was my fault, and I'll never be able to live that down. Yet things were getting serious around Albany, and I carried my gun wherever I went.

I telephoned Gypsy a few times, but I only got her answering machine again. She must have been out on the streets, selling her body for crack, another vicious cycle of her sickness. All of Albany was sick in this way, the poor areas pushing out to the suburbs, the opioids, the heroin, the cocaine, the meth, the pot, pushing out with them. Albany was like a station where drug dealers stopped and sold their wares. It was a fierce open-market. It was competitive. I could just feel the presence of our neighborhood expanding, the cops arresting people, the dealers running from them. And then there were the casual users, some of whom easily turned into addicts.

After three or four times, they needed to get high while blanketed by insanity, fear, and poverty. These substances always dragged them to the grave, no matter what they looked like. It was just so terribly sickening, and yet not a person I knew told me that these addicts were to blame. It developed into a tried and true machine of making money, while resting assured that full-blown addicts would soon die in its gears.

But I had to get rid of my supply, since I was taking a break from the business. I didn't want to flirt with danger. I didn't want to play with fire. Yes, we made a lot, and what I made should have lasted me for the rest of my life and double that, enough for two lives, but I could no longer pretend. It was either jail or death, and I wanted Gypsy to leave Albany with me. Just dart off to the Caribbean with her and rest from severe exhaustion and a re-tinkering of our plans. I guess I still wanted a family. I wanted that family to be with her.

That night, though, when I stopped by my wholesaler's place to give him whatever supply I had left, he wouldn't let me in. He opened the door slightly. He was in a luxurious Turkish bathrobe and slippers. And then I heard a familiar voice calling to him from inside the bedroom.

"Now's not the time, Charlie," he said.

"Sorry for bothering you," I said. "I just wanted to drop off whatever I have left."

"Smart move, getting out while you can."

"It's just too dangerous. The woman in your bedroom, though. The voice sounds familiar."

To my astonishment, Gypsy came to the door in a large bath towel wrapped around her ever-increasingly thin, reedy body. I took the gun from the slip of my back and pointed it at the both of them.

"Now, Charlie, just relax, okay?" said my plug. "Why don't we start by putting the gun down, okay?"

"I'll kill you both right here," I said, tears beginning to gather.

"Charlie," said Gypsy, "will you put down the gun? Let's talk this out."

"God," I said, "you really are a whore, aren't you? After all we've been through together, you're actually sleeping with my fucking plug? I can't even think of a punishment harsher than pushing me away all the time and then sleeping with him. But I still do want to marry you, Gypsy, but first I'll have to kill this asshole to stop him from sleeping around the whole city of Albany."

"Just put down the gun," said my plug. "This was just for one night, I swear it. She's just a whore, Charlie. She was just someone to fuck. She's just someone to suck a dick. She goes around town fucking everyone – niggas, spics, you name it. She's a filthy whore, Charlie. She'd fucked most of the police. She's fucked most of the niggas in Arbor Hill and the South End. All of those black dicks in her, Charlie. You don't want to kill me for telling you all this. It was just for you to know, that's all. She likes to fuck. You don't want to kill the man who introduced this to all of this, right? I didn't think about how you were seeing her too. But she doesn't want to marry you anyway."

"No, I don't," she said. "I'll never marry you, Charlie. You can shoot me right here, but I'm not in love with you. Now put down the fucking gun."

I wanted to pull the trigger on them both. The sense of betrayal that I felt was more powerful at that moment than it had been ever since I had moved to Albany and abandoned the college track in Hartford. It was then that I knew that I had to get far, far away from my plug, and now his new fuckbuddy, Gypsy. It had been enough. I vowed right then and there that I would never again involve myself with a woman such as this. Both of them had betrayed me, and I cocked the trigger as they nervously stood in front of me in the doorway.

"She's a whore, Charlie. Why are you so in love with a whore? Hell, I could find better for you. Is it because she's good in bed?"

"That has nothing to do with it," I said.

"Charlie, put down the gun, okay?"

It became much easier to believe that Gypsy wanted nothing to do with my ideas of marriage and children. She had slept with so many men that I was unsure what she wanted, and if she wanted me too.

"C'mon, Charlie," said my plug, "This is not you, man. You're a smart kid. You kill us, and you can never bring us back. You kill us, you'll have to live with it for the rest of your life. These are the streets, Charlie. It's not supposed to be easy. It is not all black and white. Look at this girl and understand that this woman in not capable of having any sort

235

of wedding with anyone. It's just sex. She's an Albany crack whore."

"Please, Charlie, put down the gun," she said. "I'll spend the night with you, no charge. How about that?"

I wiped away the tears. I knew that I would never harm these two people who had slowly taken over my life. It wouldn't be worth it. Jail, death. What happened to Cash. Where else could I go? I was stuck. Or at least it looked like it, until I thought of going up to New Hampshire to see my parents again.

I didn't want to move up a level or expand the heroin drug operation to include cops, rival gangs, and more danger. I couldn't handle it any more. I threw my gun to the floor and ran down the stairwell to safety outside. I was scared of myself and what I had turned into. How this could happen to an Exeter grad? A Trinity student? I had no idea.

I had heard several times before, though, that the kids that go to Trinity are survivors. We're always in danger, but we are also built to last. It's another type of virtue that we pull out whenever we are threatened by someone or something. We're just made that way.

I hopped into my Jaguar after a couple of days of depression to run away for good to New Hampshire again. I wanted to show them that I had made a lot of money, the only thing my family really respected. I wanted them to see that I didn't need college anymore.

Once the money was wrapped up at the bank the next morning, there was little point in going back to school or getting a stupid job. I was free of my plug and of Gypsy, and my final visit to my family's place would signify that I was going to live without them too. It was a weird time, and I would live far away from anyone who ever knew me in some weird place I didn't recognize.

The drive out of Albany was therapeutic. I listened to pop radio, and that alone made the ride somewhat bearable. I had satellite radio in the car, and the lack of any commercial interruptions also felt weird. There wasn't a break in the music, as though I had been trained to accept advertisements that put a happy smile on almost every facet of my American life. The Jaguar, though, drove like a dream.

Even though I was completely demoralized at that point, I still wanted my father to see the car, to show him that I could make the money, to prove to him that I wasn't so helpless out in the world. But when I slowly drove down a blank Central Avenue towards the tangled highways that led North, I couldn't leave without seeing Gypsy again. She was all strung-out, high on crack, selling her thin, reedy, and pockmarked body to the passersby on the street. I then sped up and made sure that I had left Albany for good this time.

The image of her tore me at the seams, but I had to leave it all behind. There was little or no cure to this cruelty. There was no exit to what I had found in Albany. And even though I drove the highways into the bitter autumn air that had filled the city so quickly after the summer had ended, I knew I could never get rid of this place to which I had traveled. I had killed Cash, and I couldn't save Gypsy. The only person I could really save was myself. Herein lied the cruelty, the existential nightmare that suddenly became the America that I had never really known.

Always the cruelty. Always the cruelty. There was no escaping it.

When I arrived at my parent's large, grassy property in New Hampshire, I kissed my mother on the cheek, and then made a beeline for my father's den. It had wide windows that displayed the natural setting that surrounded the house. He sat at his desk reading a book on the presidency.

"Come in, son," he said.

He carefully inserted a bookmark in its spine, put the book on his desk, and then asked me to have a seat. My father, when he wasn't eating the meals that my Mom made, spent most of his time in his den. It was his favorite spot in the house - in solitude and away from the world. There, he contemplated the issues beyond the small hamlets of New Hampshire.

"Dad, I want to show you something."

It took me a little while to pull him from his desk, but it sure made him proud when I showed him the new Jaguar in his driveway. Interestingly enough, though, he still wasn't satisfied. It didn't matter how much money I had. He wanted even more than that. Like the pressure he instilled in me that wanted me to progress even further. He wanted me to return to college again.

"I don't like it," he said. "Where are you getting all this money? How did you make it?"

"I've become a businessman," I said. "I made Albany a waste disposal industrial powerhouse, and I am getting paid so well that I no longer have to worry about money, Dad. Imagine that? No more worrying about money?"

"What have you gotten yourself into?"

"Nothing, Dad. I earned this money in Albany. I'm a respected citizen."

He silently examined the car.

"Have you thought about returning to college? Son, more than money, you need an education. Our whole family line has graduated from some kind of college institution. Don't you want to try again? Just to see if you can do it?"

I wanted to say that I didn't need college anymore. I had plenty of money. But he didn't respect what I had accomplished, and so, after thinking about it over the weekend, I told my Mom and Dad that I would return to college.

They looked a bit skeptical, but they agreed that I still needed a college education. They also wanted me to get married, but I knew better than that. Actually, on all of their suggestions, I did know better. Street knowledge was way too over their heads. They had little understanding of it, but when I agreed to return to college, I understood that there were some parts of the chaos of that knowledge that I no longer needed or desired.

I realized that I had to be a New Englander again - the college graduate again, a nice job, despite winning on the streets of Albany. I missed Cash. I missed Gypsy. I even missed my plug. It was over. I had returned, finally to the place from where I came.

Looking back on it all, there were things that I wasn't supposed to see. I could have killed both my plug and Gypsy, but never before did I feel like I was blessed in some way. That blessing came to me by not shooting them. I could have easily blown those two away with the gun that my plug had given me. When I look back, though, I still wanted to kill them. The idea wouldn't leave me alone.
When I continued college, the idea of shooting people still followed me. I wanted to shut it off. I tried to fight it within my own mind, to find a kind of negotiated solution, a balance,

to killing people, but little did I know, way back when, that the idea followed me all through my life, and it was the idea of shooting someone that flipped the virtues of my later actions into thoughts that I wanted to purge. I can only say that the thought of killing Gypsy never leaves me alone. And I live with myself by remembering the time I had in Albany, and how I got away with it, and also, how I couldn't marry the whore that now sold herself along Central Avenue.